BURN

GRAHAME CLAIRE

Editing And Proofreading:

Marion Archer, Marion Making Manuscripts

Karen Lawson and Janet Hitchcock, The Proof is in the Reading

Lori Sabin

Ebook ISBN: 978-1-951878-12-2

For those who burn for the chaos.

CHAPTER ONE

TEAGUE

"PEPPER IS MISSING."

The old woman's panicked voice barreled down the phone line.

"Missing?" I sounded groggy, like she'd spoken a foreign language. I'd been fired hours earlier, and apparently my brain was already sluggish at responding to emergencies.

"Did I stutter?" Miss Adeline snapped. "She was gone . . . awhile. So I went downstairs to check on her."

I waited impatiently for her to finish the thought. Instead, all I got was silence and a whole lot of tension even though we weren't in the same location.

"How do you know she's not walking other dogs?" I had no idea what time it was. I'd been sitting in this same spot for hours.

"Because Sadie, Muffy, and Ash came back. Without her."

The glass of water I held slipped from my hands. It shattered on Lincoln's kitchen's stone floor.

Her words were a swift kick in the stomach . . . and in my mind, which shifted into high gear. I pushed out of the chair, grabbed my keys, and jogged to the elevator.

"I'm on my way."

My hand shook as I pressed the call button.

Where are you, Pepper? Please be okay.

I checked the time as I stepped into the elevator. Almost midnight.

I despised that she had to be out so late. It wasn't safe. And even though I'd asked her—more like *demanded*—to not walk the dogs at an ungodly hour, she'd put me in my place.

I should've been there.

Instead, after I'd been fired, I'd wandered around the city. Furious.

I'd ignored my phone all day, needing to be alone while I sorted out what my next move would be.

The one person I'd wanted to go to, I hadn't. Because I didn't want to dump more problems on her. She already had enough.

But if I had, maybe she wouldn't be missing right now.

Please be okay. Please be okay.

The thought replayed over and over in my head as I jumped in my truck. Rushed through red lights. Swerved around the few cars in my way.

When I was a few blocks out from Grey Paws, my body tightened on high alert. I swung my eyes from side to side, searching every dark corner and alleyway.

Hoonnnkk.

Headlights blinded me and I jerked the wheel to get the truck back into my lane.

Shit.

Come on, Pepper. Desperation to find her pricked every part of me.

Anger bubbled up as I passed the black hole that used to be her park. I crept forward, shining my lights on the destruction.

It was impossible to see anything but charred heaps of what used to be. The barrels were gone, most likely in evidence at the police station.

I banged the steering wheel with my fist. "Damn it."

She's fine. She's just . . . I didn't know where she was. And my hollow reassurances to myself did nothing to calm my racing heart.

A figure lay on the ground near what was left of the bench we'd sat on only a few days ago. I slammed on the brakes and jumped out of the truck.

Ding. Ding. Ding.

The bell sounded from the cab, where I'd left the door open and the truck running. I ignored it and sprinted ahead.

"Pepper." I rolled over the heap and winced.

A dirty bearded face greeted me. Eyes that looked lost blinked open.

I let out a long sigh and patted the man's arm. "I'll get you some help, buddy."

"Why'd you wake me up?" he slurred grumpily.

"I was looking for someone." I perked up. It was a long shot but worth asking. "Have you seen a woman?" Crap. I had no idea what she was wearing.

A loud snore came from the ground. He'd passed out again.

I texted a friend who worked at a homeless shelter to get some help for the man and ran back to my truck.

I scoured the surrounding blocks of the shelter a few times but came up empty.

I wheeled to a stop in the alley behind Grey Paws. *Please let her be back.*

Bang. Bang. Bang.

My fist hurt from pounding on the door so hard.

Woof. Woof. Woof.

A frenzy of barking started from inside.

Impatiently, I waited for Miss Adeline to answer. I glanced up and down the alley, hoping to see Pepper in her overalls with a messy ponytail and that beautiful face.

I was still surprised at how quickly she'd grown to mean something to me.

The door creaked open. The barking grew louder.

Miss Adeline's sharp eye peered at me through the crack.

"Is she back?" I asked in lieu of a greeting.

She held the dogs while I shimmied inside. Ash rocketed toward me. I knelt. She burrowed between my legs and nestled against me.

I rubbed down her sides, already comforted just being near her.

"She'll be back." Miss Adeline's voice lacked the usual confidence and spark.

I prayed with all my might she was right.

"Walk me through what happened." I needed to hear it again. To see if there was anything we'd missed.

"She told me she was going to walk a few of the dogs. I told her to take her phone and be careful. I don't even know what time it was." She shook her head and looked down at her feet.

"She has her phone?" Hope rushed through me like a tsunami.

"I've called it a million times." Miss Adeline waved her cell phone. "No answer."

"Any chance you have tracking enabled for each other?"

She brightened then made an annoyed face. "She made me put that on there in case anything happened. Because I'm an old person."

I bit my lip to keep from laughing.

"She said I could track her too when I put up a fuss, but I've never done that. Is there no privacy in this world anymore?" She continued on with a bit of her snark back, though it seemed as if she was attempting to cover up her worry.

"May I see your phone?" I held out my hand, and she readily dropped her cell into my palm.

After a few swipes and clicks, I had the tracking app open. The blue dot representing Pepper flashed. I zoomed in on the map.

"She's at the park."

CHAPTER TWO

TEAGUE

ADRENALINE FUELED, I raced back to the park.

I'd just left there minutes ago. There'd been no sign of Pepper. But one thing I'd learned as a firefighter was that things could change in an instant.

Miss Adeline stayed behind with the dogs in case Pepper called the rescue or showed back up.

With her phone glued to my hand, I kept one eye on the blue dot and one on the street. It hadn't moved, but these things weren't always completely accurate. I was just grateful for any kind of clue so we could be doing *something* instead of sitting around worrying.

I stopped the truck in almost the exact same spot as I had earlier. The man who'd been there was gone. I hoped he'd made it to the shelter but was pretty sure there hadn't been time for that.

"Pepper!" Why hadn't I called for her before?

"Pepper!"

The only response was the echo of my voice in the cold night. I searched the area frantically. There was no sign of her or her phone.

Her phone.

I stilled and dialed.

It rang on my end. I craned my neck and listened carefully for a ringtone.

Rinnggg.

I ran toward the sound on the edge of the park. The lit screen glowed up ahead. Her cracked phone danced across the sidewalk. I swiped it off the ground and whirled around, frantically searching for her.

"Pepper!"

I looked under charred bushes nearby. Maybe she'd fallen and hit her head. I checked a bench a few yards away. Behind a dumpster.

I swallowed hard as I lifted the lid to the dumpster. I shined a light inside. Just garbage, thank God.

"Damn it." I threw my hands up.

Anything could've happened.

My mind went to the worst-case scenario and instinct backed it up.

I'd buy she simply dropped her phone if the dogs hadn't showed back up to the rescue without her.

That was the biggest troubling sign.

It pointed to something sinister. Something I didn't want to think about.

Bzzz. Bzzz. Bzzz.

My phone vibrated in my pocket. I yanked it out but deflated when Lincoln's name flashed on the screen.

"Where are you? We just got home and you're not here."

I plowed a hand through my hair. "Pepper's missing." I didn't want to say the words out loud. The more I spoke them, the truer they became.

"What?"

"I'm near Grey Paws looking for her." I peered into the darkness and held Pepper's phone like it was a lifeline.

"We're on our way."

Before I could protest, he hung up.

.   .   .

"SHOULD WE CALL THE POLICE?"

Beau wrapped her hands around a mug of tea and propped herself against the reception desk.

"It won't matter. She hasn't been missing long enough." I paced in front of the windows, back and forth, almost wearing a hole in the flooring.

"Anyone could've grabbed her." Miss Adeline stared at her lap.

"How are we so sure someone took her?" Lincoln asked, ever the voice of reason.

"Because she wouldn't have let go of those dogs for anything," she snapped. "And her cell phone was on the ground. I don't think she threw it there and decided to run away."

Her shoulders slumped as she sagged farther down in the chair.

Beau placed a hand on her arm in comfort. "This might be an odd question, but is there someone who might have it out for either of you? Or the rescue?"

The old woman cut her eyes to my sister. "Let's see. Our latest list of enemies could be the track in Jersey we just took all their dogs from. Or maybe that horrible inspector who's trying to shut us down. But it could've been some random crazy person."

"Has anything like this ever happened before?" Lincoln asked.

She waved her hand. "Eh. We've had the occasional threats, but mostly it's been all bark and no bite. Until recently."

Until I came into the picture.

That guy at the track was a possibility, and he would've been angry whether I was around or not.

But the inspector? The guy who made them scramble to find another place for over half their dogs?

That one was on me.

Because of . . .

"Where's Dad?" I froze and stared at my brother.

He stared back, his expression unreadable. "He wouldn't be stupid enough to kidnap Pepper."

How could Lincoln take up for him, knowing what a monster he was? Knowing what he'd done to Pepper and Miss Adeline.

"He was in his office when we left," Beau said, almost apologetic. "You don't think . . ."

"I absolutely think he's capable of this." And if anything happened to Pepper because of him, I'd never forgive myself.

"What good does it do for him to take Pepper? And we don't even know for sure that she was taken."

"Are you kidding me right now?" I threw my hands up.

"I want to find Pepper too. But we need to think clearly."

Easy for him to say. I could barely think at all. My mind was all tangled up in possibilities and worst-case scenarios. Now that the seed had been planted, my father was at the center of every single one of those thoughts.

"Call him." I pointed at my brother.

He pulled out his phone and dialed without hesitation. My emotions were mixing up my ability to reason clearly. Lincoln was on my side. Always. He simply didn't jump to conclusions as he puzzled things out.

He held the device up to his ear.

We waited.

And waited.

And waited.

"He's not answering."

CHAPTER THREE

PEPPER

"WELL, WELL, WELL. SHE'S AWAKE."

The voice sounded far off in the distance.

I blinked my eyes open and found I was still shrouded in darkness.

Are the dogs okay?

For a moment, I listened. No dogs barking. No hushed whispers. No footsteps.

Only silence.

Please let them be safe.

I prayed Muffy, Sadie, and Ash had escaped unharmed and made it to safety.

The dark was disorienting. I had no concept of time and very little of the space surrounding me.

My hands were on my lap. I moved them, expecting resistance yet finding none. I stretched my legs and found the same.

I wasn't restrained.

With my newfound freedom—sort of—I tugged on whatever was over my head.

Dim light blinded me.

I squinted, impatiently waiting for my eyes to adjust.

The floor was concrete and cracked. I was seated in a metal chair.

It was impossible to see beyond the circle of light illuminating the immediate area surrounding me.

Click. Click. Click.

Footsteps approached. Dress shoes with tassels were visible first. Then the suit pants and a long cashmere coat.

And the face that was so familiar yet a stranger.

I was stunned once again how on one man these features meant protection and security, while on the other they were terrifying.

"I don't like that it's come to this."

I snorted. Samuel Hollingsworth seemed to thrive on intimidation.

"Let's not bother with innuendo."

I remained silent as he stepped closer. One half of his face was bathed in light, the other in the dark.

"You're in a unique position, Pepper." Something about the way he said my name sent a chill skittering down my spine. "You alone hold the power to get me what I want."

He walked a slow circle around me. I sat statue still, hoping I'd wake up and this would all be a nightmare.

"But I too hold the power to let you keep what you want."

Thump. Thump. Thump.

My heart beat so loudly in my ears I could hardly hear his voice. I had zero doubt he'd take away everything I loved without a second thought. He'd already proven that, considering over half my dogs weren't at the rescue anymore.

He stopped in front of me and looked down. He tilted his head, those sinister eyes inscrutable.

"Interesting you haven't asked me what I want," he mused, almost as if he were curious as to why.

"I'm pretty sure you're going to tell me. Otherwise, this whole charade would be pointless."

He glared, and I tried not to shrink into the chair. And then he laughed.

The sound vibrated and echoed throughout the cavern.

He shook his finger at me. "I see why he's drawn to you. His mother had that same spirit."

Then he clamped his mouth shut as if he'd spoken out of turn. Or did the mention of his dead wife affect him in the same way it did Teague? It seemed impossible this man was capable of any sort of feeling, but even monsters could be wounded, couldn't they?

"You're going to convince my son to come to work for me."

"If you changed your tone, you probably wouldn't need me to do that." *Pepper.* I excelled at keeping my mouth closed. My fingers trembled despite sitting on them. Yet I appeared determined to piss this man off.

"And when you do," he continued as if I hadn't spoken, "I'm going to let you keep your little mutt house."

The vision of him kicking Muffy blasted into my brain. How dare he treat my dogs that way, let alone speak of them like that?

"Teague is his own man. Not to mention he already has a job."

I should be agreeing to whatever his father wanted so I could keep Grey Paws and move on with my life.

But I didn't trust him.

"I am not a man you want to toy with."

"I'm aware of that, but I'm afraid you think I hold some power that I don't." *Why am I still sitting here? Why didn't he tie me down?*

He went to the trouble of kidnapping me yet didn't seem to be holding me prisoner. *He's a master of mind games.*

"For your sake, you should hope you hold that power. If you don't, I have no reason to . . . show mercy."

Fear and anger propelled me to my feet. "I have nothing to do with your family drama. Leave mine out of it."

I stormed in the opposite direction of where he stood, hoping there was a door.

"Oh my dear, how wrong you are." His voice stopped me when I'd reached the shadows. "Did Miss Adeline tell you about her recent visit to her physician?"

What visit?

"Hmm. I didn't think so. Wouldn't it be a shame . . . well, you should probably discuss it with her."

I couldn't move. Was he lying? Or worse . . . was he telling the truth?

"And don't think you fooled anyone regarding the whereabouts of those other mutts. I have to hand it to you. Daniel Elliott isn't someone I want to cross, but rules are rules. I hear the city shelter is intensely overpopulated. How many animals do they exterminate a day?"

A violent trembling rattled my core. Whether or not he was being honest about Miss Adeline didn't matter. I understood every unspoken syllable.

He'd hurt my family.

He'd hurt my dogs.

He'd hurt my friends.

And he'd do God knew what to Teague.

This man redefined the word manipulation.

"And Pepper?" I closed my eyes. This couldn't be happening. "You will make sure my son is my employee within twenty-four hours. It's mind-boggling how many accidents happen these days . . . to the elderly. To animals. Safety is such an illusion."

CHAPTER FOUR

PEPPER

BROOKLYN.

He'd taken me to Brooklyn with no money or phone to get back to Grey Paws.

It was late. I had no idea where a subway station might be, and there wasn't a cab in sight.

Twenty-four hours.

I had twenty-four hours to convince Teague to go to work for his family business.

Or I would lose everything.

And I couldn't do either.

How was I supposed to tell him the position his father had put us in? He'd quit the job he loved for me and the dogs.

Everything he'd done proved he'd make the sacrifice.

I couldn't let him be miserable for us.

But if he didn't, where did that leave Miss Adeline and me and Grey Paws? Teague's father had already divided us. He took me tonight. What else was he capable of?

And why? What wouldn't he stop at? What accidents? *Crap.*

You could run.

I leaned against a light pole.

For twelve years I'd had a home. Could I pack up the dogs and Miss Adeline and find somewhere to start over?

I kicked at the pole.

Why should we be the ones to give up everything?

We'd worked hard to build the happy life we had. And we were happy.

Of course we could have that anywhere. But we had it here.

I just wasn't sure how to keep it.

I pushed forward with determined steps.

The last time I'd run, it had been easy. I'd been embarrassed, humiliated, ashamed, and it wasn't hard to hide from that. In fact, disappearing had been easy, but cowardly.

Leaving everything hadn't mattered because I'd had nothing left.

Now, there was so much to lose.

And what guarantee did we have that Teague's father would keep his end of the deal?

None.

What would be the next hoop to jump through? Not that I'd dealt with anyone like that man, but for people like him, there was never enough. We'd just keep giving and giving until there was nothing left.

"We need a miracle." I spoke softly to the sky, hoping someone or something would hear me.

I'd been saved before by Miss Adeline. Was I out of favors? Or did I have another hand to play?

A dull throb pulsed between my temples. Whatever they'd given me to knock me out had almost completely worn off. I had no idea if I'd been gone for hours or days.

But I needed to be home.

To see Miss Adeline.

The dogs.

Teague.

Guilt that he was in this horrible position washed over me. Why wouldn't his father just let him live his life?

Up ahead, a staircase leading down to the underbelly of the city appeared. I quickened my steps in hope.

The subway.

I jogged down the steps. The station was deserted, so I hopped over the turnstile and promised myself I'd pay back the fare later.

I BOLTED from the Eighteenth Street station. The sky was still pitch black save a few clouds and stars.

Relief coursed through me at being back in a familiar space.

I raced down the sidewalk as fast as my feet would carry me.

Almost there. Almost. There.

I rounded the corner and flew toward safety. Toward home.

As I grew closer, I noticed that all the lights were on. A figure moved inside.

And then paws landed on the window.

The bark I loved so very much was such a sweet sound.

I'd made it.

Home.

CHAPTER FIVE

TEAGUE

WOOF. *Woof. Woof.*

Sadie jumped, placing her big paws on the window. She threw her head back and barked.

"It's not time yet," Miss Adeline said.

That dog had a built-in clock for mealtime.

I checked my watch. A little after five.

It would be daylight soon, and there was still no sign of Pepper.

Sadie dug at the glass. Her nails slipped on the surface, and her barking grew more intense.

I moved beside her and glanced out the window.

"What's got you so stirred up?" I touched her head, though that did nothing to calm her.

I squinted.

Something moved outside.

I blinked, uncertain if I was just seeing what I wanted to see.

The barking faded to the background. I touched the window.

The shadow drew closer.

It looked to be the right height.

When it almost reached the door, I threw it open.

"Pepper."

She rushed inside, but I caught her fearful look over her shoulder before the door closed. What had happened to her?

Sadie barreled toward her, almost knocking her down. The dog whimpered and squealed in a way I'd never heard from her before.

Pepper knelt. Sadie attacked her with kisses. And then she was surrounded by the other dogs, who all wagged their tails and swiped at her face with their big tongues.

Pepper laughed and petted whatever wiggling greyhound body she could reach.

I tried to see if she was hurt. By all appearances she seemed okay.

Miss Adeline stood and ambled to the giant pile.

Pepper stood and threw her arms around the old woman. They hugged for a long time with eyes closed.

When they finally broke apart, Miss Adeline held her at arm's length.

"I'm okay," Pepper whispered. "Looks like they are too." She pointed at the dogs with her chin.

"Don't ever scare me like that again." Miss Adeline shook Pepper.

"I don't plan to."

Beau glided over, apparently giving them all the time together she could stand. She yanked Pepper in for a hug. "What happened?"

"Who did this?" Lincoln asked.

She'd yet to look at me.

I wanted to take her in my arms. Feel that she was safe and *here* despite that I could see she was.

There seemed to be a chasm between us. One that was palpable. One that I wanted to erase.

"Are you hurt?" I asked hoarsely.

She shook her head, but still she refused to look in my direction.

"What happened?" Beau asked again, this time more gently and less urgent.

Pepper squeezed Miss Adeline's hands. "How did you find them?"

Naturally, her first concern was the dogs. It always was. That was one of the reasons I admired her so much.

"They showed up back here. Without you." Miss Adeline spoke

quietly. There was almost a silent question at the end of her statement. The one Beau had already asked twice.

"They tried—" Pepper's voice caught, like she didn't want to think about what had led us to this point.

"Should we call the authorities?" Lincoln asked, phone in hand at the ready.

"No," she answered quickly. She stooped once more to pet Sadie. Her comfort crutch. "I appreciate all of you being here, but I'm exhausted."

"Of course, you are," Miss Adeline said before any of us could protest.

Part of me wanted Pepper to get the rest and recovery she needed. The other part was desperate for answers.

I glanced at Lincoln, who shook his head. *Don't push it.* He didn't have to say it. I understood completely.

"Can I make you some tea?" Beau asked. She didn't get the message to let Pepper be.

"No. Thank you, though. All of you." Her slight smile was tired but genuine.

"I'll walk you up."

Finally, her eyes met mine. "I'm good."

I didn't want to let her out of my sight. "I'm not."

She released a long breath of acceptance and moved toward the stairs.

"Rest well. We'll be here when you need us," Beau called.

Pepper turned and nodded.

We were quiet as we trudged up the steps. Sadie, Muffy, and Ash were right with us, their nails clicking on the hardwood.

I followed her wordlessly through the apartment. She shrugged off her coat and laid it over a kitchen chair. Her overalls had a dirt streak down the leg. *Not* one caused by a dog paw. Her hair was a mess with strands of it loose from what was left of her ponytail.

She looked the same if not a little worse for the wear. But she looked different. All the things I adored about her were in place, yet I felt the invisible barrier between us.

"They can be . . . a lot," I said when we reached her room.

She sat on the edge of the bed and tugged off her boots. They landed with a thud a few feet away. Sadie jumped up and made herself at home on the pillows. Her watchful gaze was glued to Pepper.

Ash stayed beside me, and Muffy stood next to the bed close to Pepper.

"You all shouldn't have worried. I'm fine," she brushed off, back to looking anywhere but at me.

"Miss Adeline called me. I've never heard her like that."

Pepper swallowed hard. "I didn't mean to scare her." She lifted her gaze to mine. "You were right."

Bitterness laced her words.

"About what?" I didn't give a damn about being right or wrong as long as she was here and safe.

"Walking the dogs late at night. It's dangerous." Her tone was robotic.

My stomach knotted. "Tell me what happened," I whispered. *Where have you been? Did someone take you? How did you get here?* These were the questions I was yelling on the inside. She didn't look harmed physically. A little dirty, but no bruises or cuts. But she'd been gone all night. She'd looked frightened. And yet didn't want the police involved. Why? *Something* had happened.

"What would you choose? In a perfect world."

I blinked at her, confused by the question. "I don't—"

"If you could pick any life, what would yours look like?"

I stared, completely caught off guard by the question. She waited expectantly, tugging on the straps of her overalls.

The truth was—I liked my life. Yeah, I'd love it if my mom were here and if I had a better relationship with my father. And I wished Beau lived closer . . . preferably the same continent. But I loved my job —my old job.

In all the chaos, I'd temporarily forgotten I'd been fired.

What did I have left besides my brother and sister . . . and Pepper?

Because it was starting to get difficult picturing my life without her. When I got that call from Miss Adeline, I'd never felt panic like that. While we waited, I'd never been more helpless.

I leaned on the dresser. Ash sat on my feet.

"I'm not sure. Other than a few things, I'm happy." I sounded uncertain, like I needed more time to think things through.

"I *am* sure." She reached for Sadie with one hand and Muffy with the other. "I have the life I want."

"Pepper . . ." What she said made no sense. I understood the words and what they meant, just not how they fit into the context of the moment.

"I have a decision to make. And I'd like to sleep on it. Unfortunately, this one"—she pointed at Sadie—"is going to start barking in oh, about half an hour."

And then I saw it. How tired and weary she was.

I was sick of the distance between us.

I pulled her into my arms. She dropped her forehead to my chest and didn't resist me.

For the first time in hours, I took a full breath.

"Don't worry about the dogs. You rest."

"I don't have that luxury," she mumbled. "And I'm guessing you've been up all night too."

"I'm used to it."

She sagged against me as if her body was finally giving out. I rubbed my hand up and down her spine, torn between angry that she had to deal with this and thrilled she was back where I wanted her. Needed her.

I didn't know exactly what was happening between us, only that I couldn't stay away. Didn't want to stay away.

And tonight . . . I couldn't remember being so scared. I wasn't sure what that meant or where this was going. While I seemed to be growing more certain in my feelings, Pepper seemed to be pulling away.

"Tell me about the decision you need to make," I said against her hair. Even if I couldn't fix my own life, maybe I could help her sort out hers.

She stiffened but didn't let go of me.

"You can talk to me. About anything," I said after she didn't speak.

When she finally looked up at me, there was so much trouble on her features I could hardly stand it.

"I'm not ready yet."

Disappointment I hadn't expected sank into my gut. It stood to reason I wanted her to trust me. Apparently, she wasn't ready to lean on me.

"Whenever you are—"

"I know." She placed her hands on my stomach, and for a second I thought she was going to push me away. "Why aren't you at work? Didn't you have a twenty-four-hour shift?"

While I appreciated her concern—no, I more than appreciated it— I wasn't ready to say the words out loud. I could barely think them. And I didn't want to worry her with things out of her control.

"Maybe it's time I thought about a new line of work," I said offhandedly. Maybe I didn't want to burden her that I'd been fired, but I also didn't want to lie either.

She jolted. "But you love your job . . . don't you?"

I slid my hand into her hair. "Yeah. Most of the time."

She tilted her head to the side.

I kissed her forehead. "Rest. We'll talk later." It was killing me not to know where she'd been, why she'd disappeared. I needed the truth, even if I didn't like it.

Her brow creased. Deep-set lines cratered around her eyes. "Monsters are real."

CHAPTER SIX

TEAGUE

CLICK. *Click. Click.*

Ash trotted down the steps beside me.

I'd been torn between staying with Pepper and letting her rest on her own. I sensed she needed a minute to herself to digest whatever had happened to her.

But it was making me crazy with worry and curiosity.

Three faces jolted in my direction.

"What happened?"

"What'd she say?"

Lincoln and Beau spoke at the same time. Miss Adeline was quiet, knowing Pepper better than any of us.

I lifted a shoulder and lowered it helplessly.

"She'll talk about it when she's ready," she said as she slumped into her chair.

The woman had been up all night too. All this stress couldn't be good for her.

"You must be tired—"

"Is that your polite way of telling me I look like death warmed over?"

Maybe it wasn't appropriate, given what had happened, but I smiled, grateful for a moment of normalcy.

"No. It's my way of saying I'll take the early shift." I winked.

"You're lucky you're handsome." She pointed an old, crooked finger at me before she stood. Then she stepped in front of me and cupped my face. "I'm glad you're around."

I was too. I hadn't realized how much until tonight.

"You just don't know him that well," Beau chimed in.

"We'll have to do something about that, won't we?"

I kissed her cheek. "Any special instructions?"

"Feed Sadie first." She started up the stairs.

"She's upstairs with Pepper."

"That dog will be down for breakfast. Mark my words."

Once she disappeared, my brother and sister surrounded me.

"What did she say? Word for word." Beau shoved at my shoulder.

I appreciated that she cared so much about Pepper too.

"Not much of anything."

Beau narrowed her eyes. "Was she kidnapped?"

I dropped into the chair Miss Adeline had vacated. "I don't know."

"Where was she?" My sister sat on the desk beside me.

"I don't know."

A growl of frustration that matched how I felt came from her direction. "What do you know?"

"Nothing. She basically said she has a decision to make and that monsters are real."

Ash put her head in my lap. I hadn't realized how much I needed her comfort.

"It was him."

Beau and I snapped our heads toward Lincoln. He shoved his hands in his pockets.

"Do you know any other monsters?"

His question was loaded. There was nothing our father wasn't capable of, but this?

I shot out of the chair. "Will you two stay with them for a while?"

Lincoln put a hand on my shoulder when I was almost to the door. "Think this through."

I spun. "Think what through? He kidnapped Pepper and did who knows what to her."

All I saw was red. Anger pulsed through my veins like a living and breathing thing.

"If you go to him, what are you going to do?" Lincoln's grip tightened. "This is what he wants from you. A reaction."

Oh, I'd give him a reaction all right.

"She didn't tell you it was him," Beau said quietly.

"Are you defending him?" I asked incredulously.

"No." Her answer was quick. Insulted. "I'm saying not to be rash."

Lincoln and I stared at her. Who was this woman and what had she done with our sister? Rash was her middle name.

"When it comes to him, we have to think carefully," she said, almost defensively.

Lincoln sighed. "She's right."

"If he kidnapped Pepper . . . if he did anything to her, there's nothing to think about," I said through gritted teeth.

"So what's the grand plan? Are you going to abduct him?" Lincoln still hadn't unclamped his hand from my shoulder.

"If I have to." I lifted my chin.

"Consider Pepper and what's best for her," he argued reasonably.

"I am," I shouted and immediately regretted when the pile of sleeping dogs all lifted their heads in unison. "Sorry," I mumbled.

The pitter-patter of paws on the steps caused us all to look in that direction. Sadie trotted over, looked up, and proceeded to bark. And bark.

"It's that time, huh?" I scratched behind her ears and followed her to the back.

Beau and Lincoln were right behind me.

"How does this work?" Lincoln shrugged off his suit coat and hung it on the rack of leashes.

I glanced at the empty kennels and then to the turned over bowls on a towel next to the sink.

I fed Sadie so we could communicate without shouting.

"Fill these with water and put them in each kennel," I said, handing them a stack of bowls.

"Food's in here, right?" Beau stood next to the refrigerator.

I nodded and grabbed the large container while she held open the door. I was so grateful she knew where things were. She might not live in the States but since she'd met Pepper, she'd basically commandeered best friend status.

Lincoln pointed to the glass container with his chin. "I thought dog food came in a bag?"

"Not this dog food," Beau said haughtily. "Lexie is a genius. And a humanitarian. Or dogitarian."

"I'm not even going to ask." Lincoln continued filling bowls with water.

Sadie finished her breakfast, took a quick look to make sure I was doing everything correctly, and then scooted back upstairs. To be with Pepper.

"Why is Dad bothering Pepper?" Beau asked.

"Because of me," I answered quickly. I paused mid-scoop, hating I'd brought her onto his radar.

"What does he want from you?" She distributed a bowl of food.

"I honestly have no idea." And I didn't.

We hadn't gotten along since Mom died. He'd made basically no effort in attempting to have a relationship with me beyond trying to rule my life. But I didn't even know why he wanted to do that.

"He wants you to come to him, and he's using Pepper to get to you," Lincoln said. "And you almost played right into his hands."

I hadn't yet ruled out paying him a visit. But once again, I was glad Lincoln had stopped me from going in with blinding anger to a situation out of my control. I needed a clear head when dealing with him. I couldn't afford any missteps.

I passed another bowl to Beau. "How do I get him to leave her alone?"

"You aren't one hundred percent sure he had anything to do with this," she said, taking it from me. "It looks bad, but it could be a coincidence."

I flashed her an unimpressed look.

Muffy jetted into the room from upstairs and jumped on Lincoln. Water splashed all over the dog and Lincoln's pants. *Crap.*

My brother set the now mostly empty bowl on the counter and looked at the mess. Muffy placed a paw on his thigh, and I winced, hoping he didn't tear a hole in Lincoln's pants.

I had no idea how he'd react.

He stared at Muffy.

Thump. Thump. Thump.

His tail hit Lincoln's shoe every time it wagged.

He snapped and pointed to an empty kennel. Muffy obediently trotted in.

Lincoln grabbed a bowl of food and set it down for Muffy. "Your name should be Jumper, not Muffy."

Beau and I exchanged wary glances. Our brother had a good heart but liked things just so. Spills and messes and soiled pants weren't his thing. And yet, was that softness I detected?

"I saw that," he said. *Because you have eyes in the back of your head.* "And let me handle Dad."

I wanted to take him up on the offer. Badly. But if I kept doing that, we'd all end up back exactly where we were.

With our father squarely in control.

"Want to walk some dogs with me before you have to report to work?" I deflected because I was tired, couldn't think clearly, and needed a minute to decide what I was going to do.

Beau grabbed a couple of leashes. "Is there a trick to this?"

"Beats me." Pepper made it look so easy.

It took a few tries, but she got one of the dogs looped and ready to go.

Muffy stood by Lincoln like a statue. My brother dropped the leash around his neck with no problem. Once it was on, Muffy yanked toward the back door. Lincoln stumbled forward and scowled but didn't complain.

Ash gave me no trouble, allowing me to put the leash on and patiently waiting for me to lead.

It wasn't pretty, but we made it outside. Muffy did his business fast and looked up at Lincoln.

"Why is he staring at me?" my brother asked warily.

"He wants a treat."

He looked at me incredulously. "I don't have any."

I dug in my coat pocket and handed him one. Muffy jumped on Lincoln.

"Off." His voice was authoritative. Unfortunately, Muffy didn't understand . . . or pretended not to.

Lincoln kept the treat secured behind his back. Muffy put all four paws back on the ground, waited a second, then circled my brother. He nudged Lincoln's fist.

Beau and I took the scene in, trying not to laugh.

"He did what he was supposed to do," I said.

Muffy pawed at his hand, growing impatient. Lincoln snapped and pointed to a spot in front of him.

Muffy sat.

Lincoln gave him the treat.

Muffy pawed him for another.

"Demanding, aren't we?" He adjusted the leash.

I put my fist against my mouth to keep from laughing. Lincoln wasn't amused.

Muffy headed back toward Grey Paws.

Beau grinned gleefully. "You two are a perfect match."

As busy people, we rarely had time together like this as siblings working together, and despite the stressful circumstances, I was truly thankful for this moment with them.

CHAPTER SEVEN

PEPPER

THE BED DIPPED.

A gentle hand brushed my hair back.

A wet tongue licked my cheek.

I pried my eyes open.

Miss Adeline sat on the edge of the bed, looking tired. Sunlight streamed into my room, bright and cheery as if last night hadn't happened.

"What time is it?" I stretched and yawned. Everything felt heavy. I wanted to go back to sleep. Back to yesterday morning when life looked promising and nothing seemed impossible.

"A little after ten."

I squeezed my eyes shut. I'd only been asleep a few hours, but it was a luxury I couldn't afford any longer. There was too much to do . . . including to check on our dogs at the Elliotts'.

"They're fine." Miss Adeline touched my face. "I just spoke to Vivian. And Daniel."

What she didn't say was that she'd filled them in on what had happened. She didn't have to. It was in her posture.

My body relaxed and seized at once. We'd always solved our problems with little outside help. I couldn't get used to others chipping in when I fell short. I was grateful and still uneasy about that.

And I wanted our dogs back under one roof.

I wanted normal.

I wanted peace.

I wanted a shower.

None of those things seemed possible in the near future.

"What happened?"

Miss Adeline was the most confident person I'd ever known. When life got hard, she never got down. She always promised things would be okay, and they always were. But she hadn't said those words one time since I'd come back in the wee hours of the morning.

"I'd prefer you didn't go anywhere by yourself for the time being," I said wearily.

"I'll take Mr. March as my bodyguard." Finally, there was a hint of normalcy.

"Only Mr. March? I thought for sure you'd need at least January, February, and maybe July." One corner of my mouth lifted.

"August. I need August too."

I laughed before Teague's father's words came back to me. "Did you have a doctor's appointment recently you didn't tell me about?"

"I do lots of things I don't tell you about." She shifted her eyes away.

"Doctor's appointments shouldn't be one of them."

"You worry too much." She stroked my forehead again. "What did he want?"

I closed my eyes. Did I let her get away from avoiding my question? Was she hiding something, or had Teague's father planted seeds of worry for no reason?

Every bit of the anxiety I'd brought home came crashing back. It was as if I'd had no rest at all. I didn't feel more clearheaded. If anything, I was more confused.

And time was running out.

"Do you think he can be trusted?" I kept landing on the same answer but wanted to hear Miss Adeline's wisdom.

"Teague? Yes. His father?" She wrinkled her nose. "Not a chance."

She'd confirmed my worst fears.

"How do you get rid of a menace?" I rubbed Sadie's back, who was peacefully snoring.

"I asked Teague if he was ready to make his stand. Are you ready to make yours?"

For Miss Adeline and the dogs, there was nothing I wouldn't do. Did that include putting Teague in a terrible position possibly for no reason? There was no guarantee his father wouldn't come after us anyway.

"I don't know how to fight him." I slapped the side of the bed. "I don't even know *why* we're fighting him."

"The person to best answer that is sitting downstairs."

I sat up a little. "He's still here?"

"Out like a light, but yeah. Still here."

My stomach did a nervous flip. I didn't want to tell Teague what had happened. He'd do exactly what his father had asked. And I couldn't allow that. I just wasn't sure how to stop it. And I also wasn't sure why this fight was on our doorstep. It had always been Miss Adeline and me simply fighting alone for our dogs. Yet somehow, Teague had broken into our unit, bringing added strength. And now, added risk. But for a while, it had felt good to have another person shouldering our drive with us . . .

"Take a shower before you see him." She winked.

And I was never more grateful for that sassy attitude than now.

"Woman . . ."

She stood and pulled the covers off me. The cold air was motivation to get out of bed.

She paused in the doorway. "I always tried to take on everything myself, but it was the darnedest thing. Whenever I worked with my Hastings, the outcome was better."

She disappeared, but I got her message loud and clear.

Talk to Teague.

CHAPTER EIGHT

TEAGUE

"HEY, SLEEPYHEADS."

Was I dreaming? Pepper sounded normal. Happy.

Ash's body wiggled against mine.

I opened my eyes.

Pepper petted Ash's head with a secretive smile on her face. "Think she's trying to make sure you don't go anywhere?"

I looked at the dog in my lap. The last thing I remembered was sitting in the chair and her jumping up with me. It was awkward, but she was content.

"I wish she wasn't the only one."

Pepper winced.

I snapped my mouth shut. It was too forward, even if it was the truth. And I was almost past the point of caring. But I didn't want to push Pepper away.

"I don't want to tell you about last night." She propped on the edge of the desk.

"Did he hurt you?"

She shook her head. "No."

My worst fears were confirmed when part of me had hoped I was wrong.

He was responsible.

My father.

"What does he want?"

If it was my attention, he had it. I tapped my foot in rapid succession. He'd gone too far. Again. Bothering me was one thing. Harassing Pepper? Completely another.

He was quickly dismantling her life.

I didn't know how to stop him, only that I had to.

She reached down and placed a hand on my knee to still me.

"I'm sorry," I said hoarsely. For dragging her into my mess. For disrupting her normal. For not being there to protect her.

"You have nothing to be sorry for." And she sounded as if she genuinely meant that. Even if it wasn't the truth.

"He could've killed you."

Ash popped her head up at my raised voice.

Pepper recoiled. "Is he . . . capable of that?"

I plowed a hand through my hair. "I honestly don't know. I've seen a car that looks a lot like his at several fire scenes lately. Ones with bodies."

The thoughts I hadn't dared let myself think tumbled out. I shouldn't burden her with this, but she was holding something back. Something to do with him.

"You think . . ."

"It's a stretch. I'm not sure it was his car. And if it was, maybe he's just watching me." There were a thousand explanations for what I'd seen. I simply wasn't sure which one was correct. But I didn't like where my mind and gut instinct were taking me.

She swallowed hard. "If he's responsible for any of it, there's no reasoning with him."

"If he's not, there's no reasoning with him," I countered.

She hung her head. Was quiet for far too long. What did he do to her?

When she lifted her eyes to mine, they were tormented. I couldn't stand it.

"I didn't realize it until I was presented with the options, but I want you to keep the life you've built. I—I care about you."

Her words washed over me like a soothing balm. I hadn't realized how much I wanted to hear them. She wasn't always easy to read. She seemed to keep me at a safe distance.

Now, Pepper made herself vulnerable. For me.

She knotted her hands in her lap. "I have to decide between your happiness and mine. There doesn't seem to be a way to do both. And I can't choose."

Gently, I placed Ash on the floor. Then I stood, planted my hands on either side of her, and leaned in.

"But I can. Tell me what I have to do so you keep everything you love."

Her face was etched with lines of pain. "I knew you'd say that. I'm not sure that's the way it works."

I kissed her forehead. "Either you tell me what I'm up against or I go in blind and pay him a visit."

"Teague, your job is your world. You have a purpose. You've worked hard to get where you are." She was almost pleading, desperate. I had worked hard for my career, but lately, more than being a firefighter had become my priority. My every thought.

"The damnedest thing happened." I brushed her nose with mine. "A dog pissed on my tire and my life hasn't been the same since."

She clutched my shirt. "Choose yourself."

I grinned at her. "If I choose myself then I choose you."

CHAPTER NINE

PEPPER

ONLY ONE PERSON had ever put me first.

Miss Adeline.

Until Teague stormed into our lives.

If his father hadn't kidnapped me, would I have ever admitted to myself that I cared about him? I was pretty sure I'd have never told him that.

He didn't even have to think about what he wanted. Deep down, I'd known he wouldn't.

But seeing his quick reaction?

That Miss Adeline, the dogs, and I were more important to him than everything he'd worked for.

I was overwhelmed.

I clutched his shirt. "I can't let you do this. We have to figure out another way."

"You haven't even told me what he wants."

His nearness calmed me and quickened my pulse at the same time.

"He wants you to work for him," I said in a rush.

"That's all?" Teague's shoulders relaxed. "He's been after that all my life."

"Today," I whispered.

"What?"

"You have twenty-four hours—well, about eighteen now—to take a job with him." It was horrible to think about, let alone speak out loud.

Teague's features darkened. "Or what?"

The words caught in my throat. I wasn't sure I could get them out. I took a deep breath. "Something happens to Miss Adeline or the rescue or both."

A bolt of hurt stabbed at my heart. What would I be without her?

Teague growled. "Nothing is going to happen to either."

He shoved off the desk. I caught his hand. "You don't know that."

He looked as if I'd slapped him. "If it takes me working for that bastard to save this place, I don't need twenty-four hours to think about it."

"But where does it stop?" I squeezed his hand, begging for the answer.

His face went ashen. "It doesn't."

"So if we give in now, who's to say he won't come back later with another demand? We'll be right back in the same position," I spat. What sort of man did this to his child?

Teague stumbled forward and flung his arms around me. I caught him in my embrace.

"Don't lose your job over this," I said.

He pulled back. "I got fired."

My eyes bulged. "When? Why?"

"Yesterday morning. And supposedly, because I showed up to help with the fire at the park," he said with disgust. "Captain's had it out for me from day one."

"Can you appeal it?" I sounded naïve because I was when it came to matters like this.

Teague was a fighter though. I couldn't imagine him just walking away from his career.

He let out a long breath. "I haven't thought about it. I spent yesterday half furious and half in a state of shock. Then last night happened, and I mostly forgot about it."

"You didn't do anything wrong," I cried. "Who do we talk to? Your captain has to have someone above him."

"A few somebodies, but I'm not sure it will help." He hung his head. "Besides, I have a new career path. The inevitable one."

"No." I straightened. "Maybe Daniel knows who could help us. He's powerful."

"If I told my brother, he'd have me reinstated, I'm sure." While sarcasm laced his words, there was truth in them too.

"Then tell him," I said insistently.

Was he still in a state of shock? Teague had no sense of urgency about this. The longer he waited, the less chance he had of getting his job back.

I shook him when he didn't answer.

"Maybe Beau has the right idea. If I get close to my father, maybe I can figure out what the hell he's after."

"Don't."

He gave me a resolved look. "I have to."

"You're playing right into his hand." I tugged harder on his shirt.

"Why does everyone keep saying that? No one knows what his hand is. *No one.*"

I deflated. He was right.

The easiest thing would be for Teague to accept his father's proposal. He'd leave the rescue alone. We could all move on.

And Teague would be miserable.

The whole situation didn't *feel* right.

I didn't live based on feelings, but I had to listen to my instincts. None of us were safe. It felt far too simple. That a man like Teague's dad would simply walk away from the menace he'd caused at Grey Paws seemed too neat. The man kidnapped me. What was his end game? Why the pressure for Teague to work for him? Why go through me? Unless that wasn't his first attempt to get Teague's attention . . .

"I should've told you all this last night. But I thought I could come up with a solution. Now we're just that much shorter on time." Everything felt heavy, like if one more thing landed on my shoulders, I'd break.

Teague brushed his thumb over my cheekbone. "You'd had a traumatic night. There's nothing to apologize for."

I searched his face. "We don't have any other choice but to do what he wants, do we?"

He sighed. "Maybe if we had more time. But no. We don't."

CHAPTER TEN

TEAGUE

"WHY ARE YOU HERE?"

I stiffened at the sound of my brother's voice. He was the last person I'd hoped to see.

Actually, I just wanted to get in, get out, and move on. Somewhere in my brain, I kept thinking maybe this wouldn't be so bad. Maybe I'd get to spend more time with Lincoln.

He fell in step beside me as I got off the elevator at Hollingsworth Properties.

"I thought we agreed you wouldn't do anything rash," he said in a hushed tone.

Was his mouth moving?

"I'm not."

He paused mid-stride but quickly caught up to me once more and grabbed me by the arm. Instead of heading in the dreaded direction, he steered me down a different hallway.

"You're only delaying the unavoidable."

He ignored me and led us to a quiet corner by an artificial tree.

"You should've called me," he hissed.

"You've already done enough." I lightly punched his shoulder. "Thanks for staying up all night with me."

He scowled. "You never have to thank me for anything."

My brother was a fraction of an inch taller than I was, but it might as well have been a head the way he looked down. Even I could admit he was intimidating.

"There's no talking me out of this." I shouldered around him.

He caught me by the arm. "Whatever you're about to do, there's no going back."

Everything inside of me sank. I'd managed to avoid this my entire adult life. My instincts screamed at me to find another way. I'd debated between getting it over with and waiting until the last second. Eventually, I'd split the difference when I couldn't come up with another solution.

"We're already past the point of no return."

My brother's hard look couldn't convince me to abort my mission.

"I'm assuming you didn't discuss this with Beau either."

I shook my head. "I hope if I leave both of you out of it, I'll take the brunt of the punishment."

Lincoln dug his fingers into my arm. "How many times do I have to tell you?"

"It doesn't work that way," I finished for him, knowing full well how he was going to end that thought.

"Don't give up your career. Not everyone has the luxury of doing something they love."

I tilted my head. What would Lincoln choose for himself if he could? As awful as it must be working for our father, I couldn't imagine him doing anything else. He'd never once mentioned a dream, even when we were kids.

Had I taken that option away from him?

He'd sacrificed all these years for me. It was time to return the favor.

"Take Me Home" by Cher blared from the pocket of my jeans. I hurried to silence it.

Burke's name flashed across the screen. I guessed he'd somehow gotten in one last ringtone change. All these years, and I still had no idea how he did it.

I'll have to call you back later, dude.

Lincoln glanced around and seemed relieved we hadn't attracted any attention. It was almost five. The office was mostly deserted. I was surprised my father allowed anyone to leave.

I pointed at him. "Don't even think about taking over ringtone duty." I had to do something to lighten the somber mood. Hearing my phone ring was like a gut punch reminder that everything was changing.

Everything.

"I wouldn't dare." Lincoln released me, a sign of acceptance. It wasn't the support I'd hoped for, but if I were in his shoes, I wouldn't support me either.

"I better get this over with."

"Stop by my office before you leave." He motioned behind him. "It's at the end of that hallway."

I nodded once. My steps were heavy as I trudged in a direction I didn't want to go.

This is for Pepper. And hopefully for Lincoln and Beau.

Would my father always win? Would this be enough?

Something I could stand to learn from him was patience. He'd been waiting a long time for this day. One I swore would never come.

Turned out he was right all along.

The reception desk was empty. Thank God for small mercies. The fewer witnesses I had to this farce the better.

One foot in front of the other, Hollingsworth.

I'd been less apprehensive the first time I'd gone into a burning building.

A fresh wave of anger shot through me. Up to this point, my life had had meaning. Purpose.

In the blink of an eye, it had all been taken away.

Or had I allowed it to be stolen?

I hesitated.

I'd been so busy playing the blame game. My father. Captain.

Had I ever really been in control at all?

Was it always leading to this?

Could I have done something differently?

I didn't know, and there was no time to figure any of those things out. Maybe they didn't matter anyway.

If you do this, you get to keep Pepper.

No one had ever said that was a component of the deal. And that was a big assumption on my part. Besides, she wasn't even mine to keep.

But there was something there. My father knew it better than I did. Which meant I'd eventually have to give her up too. *Damn it.*

I pushed the heavy door to my father's office without knocking.

I opened my mouth to speak but quickly shut it.

Did I believe in signs? If I did, this would be a big one.

The office was empty.

CHAPTER ELEVEN

PEPPER

"I'M SORRY TO BOTHER YOU."

I paced in the back room of Grey Paws with my phone pressed to my ear. A gaggle of dogs followed my every step. They'd been as restless as me all day. I'd tried to get control of my emotions, but they felt every ounce of my anxiety.

"Pepper, you never have to apologize for calling." Vivian's kind voice came through the speaker. "Although, you can't get mad when I always answer with some version of the dogs are fine."

She laughed, and I gave a half-hearted one in return.

"They aren't causing any trouble, right?" I worried my bottom lip between my teeth.

"They're inspiring new ideas. Ones we need to talk about soon."

I wasn't sure I liked her tone. The last time I heard it, I'd agreed to a fundraiser.

"I'm a little scared."

"Did I tell you we own the whole apartment building now?"

I gulped. It was massive. And undoubtedly expensive. Apparently the Elliotts had more money than I thought, not that I'd considered it much. They never treated anyone as if they were less than them.

"You said you knew several of the tenants," I said, still a little dizzy that they owned an entire building in Tribeca.

"Pretty much our whole family lives here. Except the ones out in Texas, but I'm working on getting them to move to New York."

"Not a snowball's chance in hell, V," Stone called from the background.

"He has no idea how convincing I can be," she said low into the phone.

"Yes, I do," he yelled.

"Pshhh." I could picture her waving him off. "By the way, I think we should cancel the adoption event."

I abruptly stopped pacing. Muffy ran into me.

Relief I hadn't expected ran through me. "You do?"

"I want to keep all of them. I'm too attached," she wailed. "You could've warned me I'd fall in love."

Was she serious?

"I haven't exactly talked it over with Daniel, but he'll figure out they aren't leaving eventually."

I leaned against the counter. She wouldn't joke about that, would she? That was a ton of responsibility. They'd had time to see just how much, but still. I—I didn't know what to think.

"Pepper? Are you there?" Concern came through the phone at me.

"I'm here," I said quietly.

"We should've had this conversation in person." She sighed. "Sometimes I get ahead of myself."

"Sometimes?" I heard Muriella in the background.

Something that sounded like paper crumpling and then landing on a hard surface came through the line. A knot of the tension in my chest eased.

"We can discuss it further when I drop by if you're serious." The idea of Daniel and Vivian having the dogs wasn't so bad.

"Sure thing. I'm going by Paths of Purpose in a bit. Mrs. Quinn is totally on board with a resident and dog program. But we need to get your expertise on that. Assuming you want to partner with us," she said in a rush.

"Umm, yeah. We can talk about that too."

Paths of Purpose was an abused women's and children's shelter Vivian and Muriella worked closely with. I liked the idea of incorporating our dogs into their program in some capacity. It could be therapeutic for both their residents and ours. The dogs couldn't become service dogs without a lot of training, and given how they needed loving and a place to heal, they wouldn't be ready for that anyway. But they could certainly be used to provide a soft pelt to pat, a warm, if slobbery, hug for a woman needing that.

Those potential plans seemed like getting ahead of myself. Every moment felt like borrowed time. I had no idea where Teague was now, but I could admit I was scared. And clearly, given how calm Vivian was right now, she had no clue that I'd been kidnapped. Well, no one knew, because I didn't tell them. But from what Teague said, they already suspected their dad.

"Is there any news about the inspector?" I blurted.

Daniel had promised to do all he could to get the man off our backs. If that threat was eliminated, that would be a relief.

Not to say Teague's father couldn't have another one show up.

Vivian was silent. Too quiet for too long for my liking.

"Not yet. He's pulling in every resource he has," she finally said.

"Thank you."

"Samuel Hollingsworth is a powerful man. If it were anyone else, this would already be taken care of, but people have to choose sides carefully in this fight."

Because if they picked wrong, there could be big consequences. I'd already had a taste of what Teague's father was capable of. I didn't want to think what would happen if he applied more pressure.

"If you need to let this go, I understand." I fiddled with the button of my overalls. "I'm sorry I put you in the middle of this mess."

"We like being in the middle of messes," she said lightly. *Not this one.* "Ow." Her voice was muffled. "I know it's a bad situation. M said I shouldn't act so nonchalant about it. I didn't mean it that way. We're going to get through this."

"I hope so." We had to. There was no other choice.

Bang. Bang. Bang.

"Hang on a sec, Vivian."

I opened the door to the front room a crack and peeked through.

No. He couldn't be here.

Surely we hadn't already run out of time.

CHAPTER TWELVE

PEPPER

IF I IGNORED him long enough, he'd go away, right?

No matter how I shushed them, the dogs wouldn't stop barking. I couldn't even hear if the inspector was still knocking on the door.

One day of peace.

Heck, at this point I'd take a few hours.

That was a big ask.

I tossed dog treat after dog treat in an attempt to quiet the barks. I reached in the tin while keeping one eye focused through the crack.

My fingers grazed crumbs and metal.

And now they were barking because I was out of Garrison's treats.

I squinted, the metal frame of the front door blocking my view.

"Shhh." I put my finger up to my lips.

It was useless.

I closed the door and leaned against it. Teague left a few hours ago. He'd said he wanted some time to sort himself out before he confronted his father.

Now it was almost six.

Might as well feed Sadie.

At least I could use the excuse I didn't hear the door if the inspector didn't leave. That wasn't too far from the truth now.

I sent up a quick mental message to Miss Adeline to stay upstairs. As much as I'd like to see her handle that man, I wasn't totally sure exactly how she'd go about it. My guess was it might not be pretty.

Or maybe she'd flirt with him.

Nah.

Firemen were more her thing. Or was it men in suits? I'd lost track.

Bless that old woman for making me temporarily forget about the trouble on our doorstep. Literally.

BANG. BANG. BANG.

Oh no.

Someone was at the back door. I had no peephole, and there was no way I'd open it even a millimeter.

BARK. BARK. WOOF. WOOF.

The dogs rushed toward the knocking. They jumped and pawed and scratched at the metal door.

Well, this was going to be an exercise in patience.

Or I'd pass out from a heart attack.

With the way my heartbeat drummed, I'd bet on the second.

I couldn't avoid the man forever. But I wasn't ready to face whatever he had to say. Because I didn't think he'd dropped by to tell us what a great job we were doing or to see if there was anything the city could do to help us out.

We weren't perfect, but we did our best. And we didn't deserve this.

Under normal circumstances, I'd have already let the man inside. No one was playing by the rules. I had to do what was best to protect my family.

This bordered on harassment. Who was I going to call? The city would laugh at me, especially since it seemed to work based on who had the most money to grease palms.

A piece of paper slid partially under the door. Muffy jumped with both paws, attacking as if it were something to play with.

We had no idea exactly what horrors most of these dogs had been through. I marveled at their resilience. To watch them thrive after only a little love inspired me.

If only we humans could live with even a fraction of their innocent and forgiving spirits, I might not be standing statue still, pretending if I didn't move the inspector would eventually go away. But if he did, he'd be back.

I crept toward the back door, almost afraid to touch the paper. If I picked it up and he was on the opposite side, he'd know I was here and avoiding him.

I craned my neck, and my knees almost gave way when I read the words in thick black ink.

It's Lexie. I tried to call.

I corralled the dogs away from the door and opened it as she hopped into her aqua and white retro van. I waved, relieved to see the two faces who made the gourmet dog food the pups were crazy over. She waved back and jumped out.

The passenger window rolled down. "Can I come see your doggies, Pepper?"

"If it's okay with your sister, Eric."

Lexie's brother beamed at me. He practically leapt out of the van. Every day he was so enthusiastic and bright, something that certainly made this sweet man with Down syndrome even easier to love. I'd never asked how old he was, but I'd guess in his mid to late twenties. He was Lexie's sidekick, and while I didn't know for certain, I was pretty sure she was his sole caretaker.

"Hey. I wasn't sure if I stirred up the pooches for nothing." She hustled around on skyscraper heels like she had on tennis shoes. "Sorry I'm late," she said breathlessly.

Today she had on a royal blue silk jumpsuit with the collar flipped up. I'd never seen her in jeans or anything less than runway ready. More than once, I'd wondered if she made the dog food in her beautiful clothes.

She slung open the van door with ease. If I were wearing that outfit, I'd have tripped six times just going around the front. She made it look easy.

"You look sharp today." I flicked my chin toward Eric's bow tie.

"Dressed for success." He held up his hand for a high five.

"Saved the best for last." Lexie pulled out a couple of massive glass containers.

"They're going to jump on you." I winced. "Give me a sec to get them into the kennels."

"Don't be silly." She carried on toward me. "I'm all about the puppy love."

"But your outfit—"

"We go through this every time we come by," she said good-naturedly. "They're only clothes, right, Eric?"

"Right."

My interaction with them was limited to a few minutes a day. In that time, I'd never once seen Lexie treat her brother like he had a disability.

"With what I've made off Beau, I can afford a replacement." She winked.

I didn't know their arrangement, but I had the sense Lexie was donating her time and resources to feed our dogs.

And she was too pretty to hug.

I opened the door a little wider, and she and Eric shimmied through while I tried to keep any dogs from escaping. Silly me. When their noses caught the scent of what she had in her hands, they had no desire to bolt out the back door.

They swarmed her.

And Sadie was the worst.

She jumped on Lexie from behind. Lexie stumbled forward, fumbling the dishes. Fortunately, she was close enough to the counter she dropped them onto it as if she'd meant to do that all along.

"At least I know they approve of the food." She brushed a strand of hair out of her face that had come loose from where she had it pinned back.

I appreciated her good nature.

More so, right then, I was thankful for two smiling, welcome faces. I took a deep breath, trying to find calm in the midst of my latest storm.

"You know they more than approve of your amazing food, Lexie."

At least the dogs weren't distressed now but were jumping with excitement rather than fear. Food would do that. If only it was as easy to switch gears as a human.

"I have two more."

"I'll distract them since you brought their supper." I held up a bowl. "There's a doorstop if you need it." I pointed toward the floor close to the exit.

She kicked it in place on her way out, careful to make sure no one went rogue and followed her.

Sadie barked, and I tapped her nose. "We gave you the wrong name." She kept talking right over me. "Trouble. That's what we should've called you."

She trotted over to her kennel and stamped her paws impatiently.

"I'm hurrying," I said before I placed her bowl on the floor.

"Where's Milwaukee?" Eric searched frantically for his favorite dog.

She was hard to spot in the mass of bodies.

"Right . . . there." I pointed to where she stood near the back of the pack, tail going a million miles an hour.

He barreled toward her and made himself at home on the floor. "Can I have her ball, please?"

I dug in the toy basket and tossed it to him. He threw it and Millie happily fetched.

Lexie breezed back in, kicking the doorstop out of the way, and set the next delivery on the counter. A fond expression formed on her face when she took in Eric playing with Millie.

"Did you drive by the front on your way to the alley?" I asked carefully.

"Yes. Why?" She adjusted her long necklace which had gone askew.

"Was there anyone at our door?"

"I didn't see anyone." Her cheeks turned pink. "But we might've been giving a concert to ourselves."

At least our inspector problem seemed to be gone for the moment.

"Bobby McGee!" Eric cried.

"Good thing I love that song," Lexie said.

I scooped dog food into a bowl. "Do you take requests?"

She laughed. "Nope. Just Bobbie McGee."

Bang. Bang. Bang.

Her eyes rounded at the severe knock on the back door.

Not again. We'd never had that many visitors in one day. Under normal circumstances, I'd welcome them.

Bark. Bark. Bark.

If this kept up, these dogs would be hoarse soon.

Bang. Bang. Bang. Bang.

"Are you going to answer that?" Lexie asked.

"Do I have to?"

I trudged to the door and put one hand on the knob. Was I ready to face this inspector?

No. The answer was a resolute no.

I can't do it. I can't risk them. If I didn't open the door, maybe I could delay whatever was in store for them.

Lexie and Eric probably thought I was crazy.

"Pepper. Are you there? It's Lincoln."

I yanked the door open with relief . . . and surprise.

He bulldozed his way in. Muffy jetted straight for him. He held out his hand in the stop position. Muffy bumped it with his nose . . . and jumped on another of Lincoln's expensive suits.

"Have you seen Teague?" The man seemed unflappable. He'd been kind to us, but he still scared me a little.

For him to be here asking about his brother? My heart, which had barely slowed from the earlier excitement, sped up again.

"Wow. No hello or how are you?" Lexie muttered.

I recoiled. She'd never once had a snip to her tone, even when she'd been bombarded by dogs.

Lincoln glared then turned that sharp gaze to me.

"Not in a few hours." I clapped for Muffy to come. Instead, he sat at Lincoln's feet and pawed his thigh.

Lincoln absently touched his head but didn't correct him for his behavior like he usually did.

"Hi." Eric threw the ball for Millie again and waved at Lincoln.

Lincoln blinked in surprise. He parted his lips and then shut them as if he didn't know what to say.

"That's how you greet someone." Obviously, Lexie wasn't at a loss for words.

"I thought he was going to see your father?" That little niggle of worry blossomed as I attempted to defuse an escalating situation.

"Do you have a boyfriend?" Lexie tilted her head.

I got hot all over. No way was I thinking about that. Especially not in front of an audience.

"That's irrelevant," Lincoln dismissed, finding his voice again. "So Teague hasn't been by in the last hour?"

"It's not irrelevant to me." Lexie made a face. "And didn't you hear her the first time? She said a *few hours.*"

I bounced my gaze back and forth between them. The hostility was palpable.

"Who is this?" Lincoln demanded.

"Why don't you ask me instead of Pepper?" Lexie planted a hand on her hip.

His nostrils flared. "I need to find my brother." He sounded as if getting that simple statement out without shouting was an exercise in self-control.

Eric threw the ball close to Lincoln. Millie skidded toward him, but Muffy caught it first. A tug of war ensued, and Eric got in the middle of it. Muffy easily and gently yielded the ball to him.

"What's going on?" I tugged on the strap of my overalls.

Lincoln cut his eyes over to Lexie as if she weren't privy to this conversation. She folded her arms and leaned on the counter, not going anywhere.

"He came by the office and was supposed to see me after he finished . . ." It seemed the thought of Teague giving in was as unbearable for him as it was for me. Maybe more so. Lincoln understood the gravity of consequences in a way I couldn't. "They were both gone."

Everything in me went cold. Had their father taken Teague somewhere?

"Did you call him?"

I regretted the question when his lethal look fired in my direction.

"Beau doesn't know where he is either."

Realization dawned on Lexie's face. "Are you Beau's brother?"

"Not that it's any of your concern, but yes," he said shortly.

"How? She's actually pleasant."

The ball hit Lincoln's shin. Eric laughed. Slowly, Lincoln stooped. Oh no. He'd been patient—for him, at least. I hoped he hadn't hit his limit.

He scooped up the ball and tossed it. When Millie retrieved it and started to bring it back to him, he snapped and pointed at Eric. She returned the ball to Lexie's brother.

Millie was so obedient and extra gentle with Eric. She never stopped amazing me, considering she'd been left to die with a horrific dog bite at a track in Pennsylvania.

"Can you call him?"

Lincoln wasn't friendly, but something about the tone of his voice made me soften. Sometimes dogs with the biggest bark were simply hiding their wounds.

I dug my phone out of my pocket and dialed.

And while it rang, I worried. Why would his dad go through all the trouble to get Teague to work with him and then do something to Teague? This was so, so confusing.

A click from the other end of the line caused me to straighten. "Teague?"

Lincoln stepped closer. For a second, I thought he was going to snatch the phone out of my hand.

"You know what to do. Unless it's Cher. Then call right back."

His playful voice came through, but it was just a recording.

I lowered the phone and shook my head.

"He didn't answer."

CHAPTER THIRTEEN

TEAGUE

CHASING my father wasn't something I ever thought I'd do.

Yet there I was, tracking him down at the next possible place I thought he'd be.

And it wasn't a church.

I avoided this part of the city at all costs. There were too many reminders of the past. Reminders of a life that seemed as if it never existed before the pain that followed.

I parked my truck and sat behind the wheel.

Lights were on inside. Then again, they always were.

After I'd joined the fire academy, I'd never come back.

As I sat in front of my childhood home, I could picture Lincoln, Beau, and me dressed for Halloween, headed down the front walk in our costumes. And then we were older, sneaking out of this tomb that had once been so full of life. Then there was my mother.

"COME ON, SAMUEL." *Mom reached for both of Dad's hands and pulled him into the front yard. "Are you worried about what the neighbors think?"*

She grinned.

He followed her. Because he always followed her. I did too.

"Baby Don't Go" blared from the portable boom box in the grass. She sang at the top of her lungs and danced even though Dad stood still.

I flung my arms in the air and spun around in the grass. Lincoln rolled his eyes from where he sat next to Beau's carrier. I danced over to him and kicked his foot.

"Get up!" I shrieked.

He glanced at Beau, then at Mom, who twirled. Her white dress swished. She laughed when Dad caught her by the waist.

He dipped her, and his deep laugh echoed as he pulled her back up.

I dragged Lincoln to his feet. He stood there awkwardly while I moved around like a wild man.

"Let go, sweetie. Have fun," Mom coaxed as she and Dad danced.

He looked back down at our sister.

"She's fine," Mom promised.

I grabbed Lincoln's hand and tugged him toward our parents.

"Bet you can't dance as good as me," I taunted, sticking out my tongue.

Mom held out her hand to him. He took it and followed her lead as she moved.

Dad picked me up and tossed me in the air. "You're getting too big to do that." He pretended like I'd broken his back.

I squealed with laughter. "Do it again, Daddy."

I flew again. When he caught me, he kissed my head. "You'll always be my boy."

I SAT PARALYZED in my truck. The memory assaulted me from all sides. He'd erased with his ugliness most reminders that before my mother died he was loving. It may not have been natural, but she brought that out in all of us.

I didn't want to think of him as he was that day. Eventually we'd all sang Cher so loudly the neighbors yelled for us to be quiet.

That man was as much of a ghost as my mother. More like a phantom who never really existed.

Anger infiltrated the numbing pain. Mom's life was stolen from her, but our father had robbed us of a piece of our family. We'd needed him. He could've been part of what I had with Beau and Lincoln.

He wanted to chastise me about honoring my mother's memory, but *he* was the one who desecrated it. She'd be brokenhearted that I was sitting out in front of what was once our happy home, uncertain if I could go inside. Uncertain if I could be in the same room with him.

If you don't go in there, Pepper will lose the rescue.

No one deserved to lose what they lived for. What had she said to me?

"I have to decide between your happiness and mine. There doesn't seem to be a way to do both. And I can't choose."

So, I made the choice for her.

Pepper's love for Miss Adeline, for the dogs, was so heartfelt, as if she couldn't possibly live without them. She was right and she was wrong. My job was my world. It was my purpose. And yes, I had worked hard to get where I was. But suddenly, it wasn't . . . everything.

I could tolerate more pain. For her.

I shoved open the door and jogged to the front door. When I pressed the bell, muffled chimes rang on the other side of the thick wooden door. The same ones that had been there all my life.

I put my hands in my coat pockets and rocked back on my heels, barely feeling the cold. When no one answered, I used the knocker on the brass lion's head.

The door swung open wide.

"You always were impatient."

The stoic face of the man who'd been the butler my whole life filled the doorway. An unexpected rush of emotion once again rendered me motionless.

"I'm happy to let you stand in the cold as long as you like, but I'm going by the fire." Winston said in the same cutting way he'd always had.

I thrust out my hand. "You haven't changed."

He took my outstretched hand. Instead of shaking it, he pulled me in for a tight hug. "You have."

This man had disciplined me, fed me, and cared for me. When I'd left my father, I'd had to leave Winston behind too. Yet another thing he'd stolen.

Or had I given it up?

"He's waiting for you upstairs." Winston held me at arm's length.

"He is?"

"You've been sitting in your truck for half an hour." He shoved me in the direction of the stairs.

Had it been that long?

"Why are you still here?" He'd always been loyal to my father for reasons I never understood.

"It's where I belong." He motioned up the stairs. "Stop stalling."

I guessed I'd always be a kid to him, and deep down, maybe I still was.

I stood at the base of the stairway and looked up.

If I thought walking to the front door was difficult, this was like being in the belly of the beast. So many memories, good and bad, threatened to overtake me. Before they did, I took the steps two at a time.

As if I had blinders on, I refused to look at the doors to our old bedrooms, and went straight down the hall to the staircase on the opposite end of the house. I trudged up them, ever closer to my father's kingdom.

The third floor of the house had been my parents' domain. Their bedroom and my father's office took up the whole level. I hadn't come up here much after Mom died.

I swallowed hard. Her portrait was still in the same place on the wall next to my father's. She'd always said how silly it was to have a painting of herself. Somehow, my father had convinced her it was for future generations to remember her. Even after they were gone, they'd still live on in the family home.

I was pretty sure he wanted them because that was what the elite families did.

I stopped in front of the painting. As I'd grown older, I'd taken comfort in it. I hated to admit it, but my father was right. It was a way for her to have a presence even though she was gone.

Miss you, Mom.

Being here was too much stimulation. Happy. Sad. Pain. Loss. Love. All of that hit me to the point I could barely think straight.

I'd blamed my father for my absence from this place. Maybe the truth was I hadn't wanted to be here because it was too hard to take.

I strode down the hall, dread building with every step. *Would I have to come here often? Did Lincoln and Beau?*

It occurred to me that we never talked about the house we grew up in.

The door to my father's study was open.

Same chairs.

Same desk.

Same fire in the fireplace.

Same man on his throne.

Only the lines of his face were harder, and his hair had more grey.

And I became angry. Angry at the command Samuel Hollingsworth still held over me. Angry that he'd been following me. Bodies in cars. Kidnapping the woman who was my world.

And for what? Control? Subservience?

But I was a desperate man.

And that put me in the beggar's position.

CHAPTER FOURTEEN

TEAGUE

"SIT."

My father didn't look up when he spoke. I'd barely made it to the doorway. He always seemed to have a sixth sense when it came to my presence.

I was tempted to remain standing simply to defy him. Instead, I sat in one of the leather chairs across from him.

When my mother was alive, he was better about stopping whatever he was working on when we came into his space. After, he slowly became worse about making us wait.

Now, I wondered if he'd work for an hour before acknowledging me further.

It was a power play.

He hoped I'd get impatient, that I'd be the one to break the stalemate.

Too bad.

I'd sit here until I didn't want to any longer, then I'd leave. The truth was I never wanted to be here in the first place. He knew it as well as I did. Now that I'd gone all in with what I had to do, I'd do my best to win.

Although, I wasn't sure there would be any winners. If my father left Pepper, Miss Adeline, and the dogs alone for good, that would be the ultimate prize.

He closed the ledger in front of him and removed his glasses, which he set on top of the leather book. He scrutinized me to the point I grew uncomfortable.

There were no words between us. Just the thick silence full of years of anger, hostility, and pain. The emotions seemed desperate to spill over. But we'd never been two to talk things out.

What was there to say?

He was finally getting what he'd wanted all along. I'd expected him to gloat.

He didn't.

"I raised you better than to let an old woman do your bidding."

I lifted a brow, unable to stop my reaction. Old woman? I didn't know any—*Miss Adeline*. What could she possibly have come to see my father about? *Why* would she see him?

I wanted to ask all those questions and more. Instead, I crossed my legs, resting my ankle on my thigh and didn't say a word. I hoped I portrayed the image of casual indifference despite being anything but.

"I admire a woman like that. It was a fool's mission." He shrugged. "But I was tempted to show some mercy on her."

I straightened. "What did you do?"

"Do you think you can outsmart me? Have you not learned I play the long game?" He ignored my question, pretty much like he always had except when he needed something.

"And you're going to do what I want so she really was in no position to negotiate. Neither are you." His gaze was steel. I was just another adversary to him.

Not his blood.

Not his son.

"I've agreed to nothing," I said tightly.

"You're here. You wouldn't be unless you were ready to surrender." He tapped the top of the ledger. "I knew you'd come to me. I felt this culmination would be best done at home."

I narrowed my eyes. He'd left the office to lure me to this haunted house. *What is he up to?*

"Besides, you're aware of the consequences if you don't do as I wish." He waved his hand in the air. "All of this could've been avoided if you'd simply done as I asked years ago. You've displeased me."

I've displeased him?

I couldn't begin to describe how I felt in regard to what he'd done to me, and Beau and Lincoln. Abandoned. Maybe not physically, but in every other way that counted he had.

"And to think all it took was a chat with a plain dog lover." He chuckled. I saw red. But my silence should protect her. "You'll start now. In the mailroom."

Was this supposed to scare me? I wasn't afraid of hard work for little pay. And if I was in the mailroom, I'd be far away from him, so that was fine by me.

I leaned back in the chair and rested my hands around my knee. "Before I agree to anything, I have some terms of my own."

He smirked. "This doesn't work that way."

I pushed out of my seat. "Suit yourself. You've just wasted both of our time."

"You'll do anything for that girl. You have no job, which I expressed to you on multiple occasions was a total waste."

"And you know I don't need the job."

He flinched at what he knew to be the truth. The one part of our lives he had no control over.

"But you want it."

I couldn't deny it. I wanted to be a fireman again. Just because I was fired didn't mean I wasn't still one. That didn't go away.

"Why do you want me to be part of your company?" I still had no answer to the burning question. I couldn't understand the point of all this pomp and circumstance.

"Sit."

The command incensed me. "I'm not your dog."

"You're about to be."

I paced to the fireplace and nearly stumbled. On the mantel were family photos of us when Mom was still alive. And we looked happy. There was even a picture of my parents on their wedding day and one in the kitchen, my mother with her arms wrapped around my father from behind.

How could he have this photo there reminding him that he'd once been humane? Capable of love.

"She'd hate who you've become." I didn't realize my thought had been given a voice until I heard the words in the air between us.

"I've tried to get you to do what's right. There's nothing wrong with wanting all my children to work at our family business." When he phrased it that way, the notion sounded innocent enough. Never mind that he'd only been around when he wished to dictate his edicts. At least with me. I didn't really know how his relationship worked with Beau and Lincoln. Only that they seemed to tolerate him far better than I did.

"Don't put your victim spin on this." I planted my palms on the desk and leaned forward. "We're in this position because of you alone. You hate that I chose to do something other than what you wanted. I've been paying for it ever since."

"Then it's on you, isn't it? You chose unwisely," he said coolly, undeterred I was almost in his face.

The frayed thread of my control was dangerously close to snapping. I couldn't let him see he affected me, yet I was doing it anyway. It was bad enough he *knew* he did.

"You don't really want to work with me." My knuckles turned white. What was his end game?

He leveled me with a solid stare. "I very much desire that."

The words were like a shove, knocking the wind out of me. I fell back into the chair I'd refused to take only moments ago.

He was telling the truth.

"Why?" The question was barely audible, even in the quiet room.

"My reasons are my own."

The tension amped up again. Why couldn't he give me a straight answer? Was it so hard to be honest? Whatever the truth was, I wanted to hear it.

But it was useless to press him. He was a stone wall.

"I want you to leave Pepper, Grey Paws, and anything to do with it alone. If you so much as think about them, this arrangement ends. And if you can't agree to that, this is done." I was exhausted. I didn't want to screw around anymore. Being in this house was taking its toll. My father had anticipated that. He was winning.

"I won't think of them if you won't."

"No." The response was out of my mouth like a reflex.

"Very well."

One of my brows shot up. Had he conceded that easily?

"You'll start immediately. I expect you to dress and conduct your-self like a Hollingsworth."

It occurred to me the man had on a suit late in the evening as he worked from home. *Never take off the armor.*

"In other words, don't embarrass you," I said snidely.

He remained unmoved by my attitude. As if he expected it. "The standard is *much* higher for my son."

"Lincoln more than measures up."

"I was referring to you."

Internally, I jolted. He didn't treat me like a father should a son. There was no respect between us. Nothing but hatred and bitterness.

"I'm not your son anymore."

His gaze was intense as he looked at me.

"You'll always be my boy."

CHAPTER FIFTEEN

PEPPER

"THIS ISN'T LIKE him to disappear."

Beau fisted the side of her flowy skirt.

"He's not required to report his every move to us." Lincoln paced in front of the reception desk.

"You're the one who started this panic," she pointed out.

"I don't think your father would harm him." Miss Adeline had been unusually quiet all day. With all the frenzy, I hadn't had time to consider it. But she wasn't herself.

"We don't know what he's capable of," Lincoln argued.

I had an idea. But while I was in Mr. Hollingsworth's presence, I never had the impression he wanted to hurt me. Intimidate? Frighten? Absolutely.

If physical harm was his aim, he'd had the chance. Although, if he'd felt roughing me up would've made me do as he wished, he might have taken that step. Thank goodness it hadn't come to that.

Everyone jumped at the sound of Lincoln's phone. He answered in point two seconds.

He turned his back as he listened to whoever was on the other end.

"Thank you," he said before he shoved the phone back into his pocket and sagged against the desk. "He was at Dad's house."

Beau's eyes rounded. "Teague hasn't been there since he graduated from college."

The concern in her voice heightened mine.

Lincoln fished out his phone again. "I'm calling him."

"Dad?"

He rolled his eyes. "Teague."

Lincoln had been here a couple hours. Not long after he'd arrived, Beau showed up. It seemed instead of a dog rescue, we were running a search party headquarters.

I just wanted everything to go back to normal.

"Where are you?" Lincoln snapped, though he briefly closed his eyes in relief.

"Put it on speaker," Beau hissed, diving for the phone.

"On my way to the mailroom. Apparently I have to wear a suit."

I hadn't realized how worried I'd been until I heard his voice. His words gave me no comfort. He'd given up his freedom, the life he loved . . . for me.

"Don't do this," I pleaded. I couldn't let him do the thing he'd avoided all of his adult life. Miss Adeline and I would figure something out.

"It's already done." He sounded resolute with a note of acceptance.

"You're going to regret this," Beau said as she dropped her chin to her chest.

"Not if he holds up his end of the deal." There was steel in his tone.

Beau snapped her head up.

"What did you do?" Lincoln asked carefully.

"It doesn't matter." There was defeat in Teague's voice.

"You can't trust him." Desperation wove through every syllable.

"I don't have a choice. At least I'll be in the mailroom."

I hated how detached he was. That he was forced into this because of me.

"It's after eleven. Mail won't be delivered for hours."

It surprised me that Lincoln would know the inner workings of their whole company. He didn't strike me as one who'd bother with anything beyond his role. That wasn't fair. It was more like I didn't think he'd have the time. Guess I was wrong.

"And you think that matters to him?" Teague asked bitterly.

"We'll meet you there." Beau grabbed her coat and slid her slender arms into the sleeves.

"What? No. I'm fine."

Lincoln pushed off the desk. "See you in twenty."

He hung up before Teague could argue.

I marveled at the support of this family. It seemed no matter if one of them struggled, the others rallied around them. Even if that meant staying up all night working in a mailroom. And risking their father's wrath.

"I'll come with you." Teague had done so much for me. I couldn't begin to repay him, but I could try.

"No." Beau shook her head vehemently. "That's not a good idea."

"She's right," Lincoln chimed in. "We don't know why our father is so determined to close this place, but my guess is Teague's deal has squashed that for the moment. Let's not unnecessarily provoke Father."

I wanted to argue. I didn't like sitting on the sidelines when there was something I could do. But I refused to make Teague's life any more difficult than it had just become.

"Okay," I conceded quietly.

I let them out the front door and locked it behind them.

Miss Adeline stared at a spot on the desk as if in a daze.

"You've been quiet." I tilted my head. "Come to think of it, you've been absent too."

"This isn't the end, Pepper." She lifted her tired gaze to mine. "It's a temporary truce."

I plopped into the other chair. "I know."

The momentary hope that had planted itself deep within me began to evaporate. It couldn't be this simple. Teague had done what his father asked.

When would that no longer be enough to keep him satisfied?

"I went to see him."

I sat up straight. "What?"

"I thought—it was a fool's game, but I thought I could talk some sense into that man." She drummed the desk. "There is no reasoning with him."

Anyone who could kick a dog had no heart, or at least not one that wasn't rotten.

"You shouldn't have gone to see him. Not alone. Now without telling anyone." Fear fueled the volume of my voice. "He could've hurt you."

She blinked at me in surprise. I'd never yelled at her before. What she'd done was plain stupid. I don't know what I'd have done if something had happened to her.

"I had to try," she said with far more calm than I felt.

I took in a deep breath, trying to steady the turbulent emotions tossing about inside me.

"I wish you'd told me," I said once I felt a little more in control.

We were a team. We should've worked out a strategy together. But I didn't blame her for going all in to try to stop this chaos.

"Oh. This envelope came for you. With everything going on, I forgot." She offered me the overnight package.

"I haven't ordered anything," I said as I took it. "What did you offer Teague's father? You had to bargain with him with something."

She refused to meet my gaze. "It's not important. He's unreasonable."

Stubborn woman. She'd never tell me even if I interrogated her all night.

I checked the return label on the envelope.

Wood and Wood Attorneys at Law Cope, South Carolina.

A pit formed in my stomach. I tried not to think of Cope and all it symbolized very often. Only when I needed a reminder of how far I fell and how far I'd come.

My hands trembled as I stared at the envelope. I hadn't done anything illegal. Why would a lawyer send me this? *How* did anyone from Cope find me?

"Are you gonna open that? Unless they've invented something I don't know about, I don't think it's going to do it itself."

Finally, the first trace of normalcy from Miss Adeline in . . . I couldn't remember when.

"It's not an early edition of the fireman's calendar," I shot back, relaxing a bit.

"Hmph. Since you have an in, I figured I'd be the first to have one in my hot little hands." She did jazz hands, and I laughed.

"And with your in, I thought you'd be directing the photo shoot."

She pointed at me. "That's not a bad idea." She pushed out of the chair. Millie stood along with her.

"It's from South Carolina."

She tilted her head. "No wonder you didn't tear it open."

There were two people who knew I'd been homeless, but only one who knew the reason why. And the sympathy in her eyes nearly broke me.

"I'm ready to call it a night." I tucked the envelope under my arm and nudged Sadie.

She stirred, gave me a dirty look, and stretched before following us up the stairs.

When Miss Adeline reached her door, she paused. "Whatever's in that envelope changes nothing."

"I know," I said quietly. And it wouldn't as far as my life with her and the dogs.

But I had no idea if it would change my past life.

I tossed the package on the dresser.

Whatever was in there had been thirteen years coming.

It could wait.

CHAPTER SIXTEEN

TEAGUE

TWENTY-SEVEN HOURS.

That was how long I'd been up.

If it weren't for Beau and Lincoln, I'd have never made it through my first shift as a Hollingsworth Properties employee. They'd hung in with me the entire night, and there weren't words to express how grateful I was to have them.

The lack of a relationship with my father didn't matter when I had such a special one with them.

"Want a ride home?" Lincoln flicked his chin toward the car idling at the curb.

Beau yawned and climbed into the back.

"Nah."

I had somewhere else I wanted to go first.

And judging by the smug upturn of his lips, he knew exactly what I had planned. "Give Pepper my best."

"Don't come home," Beau called.

I nodded at my brother and ignored my sister.

As I strode to my truck, I realized what Beau had said.

Home.

Was she beginning to think of New York as home again? It had been cathartic to have them around. Even when they weren't at Lincoln's apartment, it still didn't feel as lonely being in my own empty place. Hell, I'd barely spent a few nights there.

Everything was changing, and so quickly. While it seemed as if most of it were for the worst, maybe it wasn't.

Lincoln and I had always been close, but we got busy. We'd go through periods where we didn't take the time we should to grab dinner or watch a ball game.

In a strange way, our father and his antics had brought me closer than ever to my siblings. We were a united front.

I hadn't realized how much I needed that reminder.

And maybe if I stayed in the family business, Beau might come back where she belonged. I was her big brother. I couldn't dictate her life. It was more likely she'd dictate mine. But she should be back on this continent. In this city. With us.

A STREAK BURST out the back door of Grey Paws. There were two dogs with a beautiful brunette in tow, headed straight down the alley toward me.

I eased to a stop and rolled down the window.

Pepper didn't seem surprised to see me.

If anything, she looked pleased.

I propped my arm on the door. "Got room for one more?"

"I know a certain four-legged creature who would be more than happy to make room for you." She spoke fondly of the dog who was quickly capturing my heart. Except it wasn't just one dog . . . or person.

"What about a two-legged one?" I grinned. Muffy jumped up and put his paws next to my arm. "I'm not interested in your wheel-wash special this morning."

Pepper snickered. "Meet me at the back door?"

"Absolutely."

I parked behind their van and hustled toward her. She'd nearly made it to the rescue. Muffy lifted his leg on a weed, and Sadie appeared annoyed.

I held the door open as Pepper ushered the dogs inside. Muffy pawed at her leg.

"Give me two seconds, okay?" she asked patiently.

"When's the calendar shoot?" Miss Adeline asked in lieu of a greeting.

Pepper's face turned scarlet.

"I haven't heard yet, but when I do, you'll be the first to know." I hated doing that calendar, but I would give anything to still be part of it now that I couldn't. Just because I wasn't part of FDNY anymore didn't mean I'd lost my brothers who could keep me in the loop.

"You do that." She wasn't messing around.

Ash dug at her kennel door and barked.

"She only does that for you," Pepper said.

Somehow that made me feel strange inside. In a good way. One I didn't quite know what to do with.

I lifted the latch, and she rocketed out. Her tail wagged when I scrubbed behind her ears. Unconditional love. That was what stood wiggling before me.

I'd never really known what that was. Ash couldn't tell me, but she'd shown me almost from day one.

And I admired the way all of these dogs gave so freely. All they wanted in return was time. Even when I hadn't given Ash that, she never held it against me.

"Can I take her for a walk?"

Pepper offered me a leash. "She'd love that."

Ash easily allowed me to loop her neck.

Sadie wandered toward her kennel despite still being on a lead.

"Oh no, missy," Pepper warned. "You didn't do anything out there."

Sadie sighed audibly and trudged toward the door, resigned to her fate.

"It could be worse," Miss Adeline said to Sadie. "You could be having a bath instead of a walk."

At the B-word, it was as if she'd pressed a button and barking filled the air.

"What's got all of you stirred up? No one is getting bath today." She might as well not have spoken. More barking continued.

"You started this." Pepper pointed to Miss Adeline. "We're outta here."

I shrugged helplessly but followed Pepper to the alley.

"Leave an old woman here with these hooligans," Miss Adeline hollered as the door shut behind us.

Pepper giggled.

Muffy pawed her again for his treat.

"You are such a good boy," she said as she fed him a biscuit.

We walked at the pace the dogs set—well, Sadie. It was barely daylight, but the sounds of the awakening city surrounded us.

"How'd it go?" Her face was pinched when she looked at me. Guilt was etched in every line.

"Better with Lincoln and Beau there." I picked up a discarded soda bottle and deposited it in a nearby dumpster. "It was busy work." I paused. "That's not fair. I'm sure the people in the mailroom have it tough, but I'm nearly one hundred percent certain my father invented a lot of what we did tonight to make me miserable."

"I'm sorry," she said quietly.

"I didn't have a good time, but it was easier when I thought about the end result."

Sadie stopped to sniff around, so we all stopped.

"I don't like this." Pepper frowned. She'd worn her stress from the moment we met, but now it was palpable.

"Hey." I grazed her cheek with my thumb. "It's going to be fine. I was out of a job anyway. When one door closes, another opens, right?"

She scowled at my pearl of wisdom. "Are you going to protest your dismissal?"

"I don't see the point. There's no expiration date on me working for Hollingsworth Properties. Even if I get reinstated, I can't go back."

Pepper kicked at a weed. "You could still have it removed from your record. So maybe you could go back one day if . . .'"

That was a big if.

But I didn't like that I'd been unfairly let go. It would follow me around no matter what ended up happening.

And I'd never backed down from what was right.

"I think I will talk to someone to appeal." The more the idea took shape, the more I warmed to it.

"Good." She looked over at me, guilt as prominent as ever. "Are you on the night shift now?"

"I have a feeling I'm pretty much at my father's beck and call." I snorted bitterly. "I'm not sure he's paying me."

"Teague." She sounded horrified. "I-I don't have a lot, but if you need some money . . ." She snapped her mouth closed.

"I'm good. But if I wasn't, I'd hit up my brother and sister. They have the big bucks." I tried to make light of it, but somehow my effort fell flat.

"Okay." Her shoulders seemed to sag in relief.

I'd get another job before I'd ever ask Pepper for a dime. And that went no matter how much money she had. If anything, I wanted to be the one to provide for her. Not that she needed me. She seemed to be doing just fine on her own.

"I didn't mean to worry you last night."

She gave a slight nod of acceptance to my apology. "Your brother was losing his mind. I was too," she finished after a pause.

I felt bad I'd concerned her, but secretly liked that she cared.

"I went to his office and he wasn't there." Anger surfaced at the thought of the games my father played. "He did it on purpose. I hadn't been to the house I grew up in since college."

She rounded her eyes. "That must have been difficult."

"It made me realize how much I have, but how much he's cost us. Not just time, but relationships too." I'd sacrificed all these years with Winston. And yeah, I'd avoided that house because it was hard, but maybe I could've found some comfort there too.

Mom loved it. She'd grown up there, and her parents had given it to her and my father as a wedding gift. There were so many good memories in that place. They could overshadow the bad if I let them.

But my father's dark cloud superseded everything.

I'd caved into him because I saw no other way out. By doing so, I'd given him power he hadn't had before. And I had zero doubt he'd be drunk on it before long.

"He wanted me to have nothing to do with you."

She froze. "Why?"

"I don't know." I shrugged. "But I told him it was a deal breaker."

She clutched the leashes so tightly I was certain the soft rope material would cut through her skin. "You shouldn't push him."

"I shouldn't let him continue pushing me around." I cupped her cheek. "He's taken away enough. I'm not giving this up."

I didn't know what *this* was. Only that little by little it was growing inside me, and I didn't want it to stop.

She leaned into my touch, silently communicating she didn't want me to give it up either. I *felt* she wanted to keep exploring what was happening between us. That she might even miss me if I weren't around.

I grinned.

"How can you be smiling at a time like this?" Yet the corner of her mouth twitched too.

I cocked my head to the side. "You like having me around."

She scowled, but it was less effective when her lips were turned up. "I fed you once and now you won't go away."

"As I recall, I fed you."

She wrinkled her nose. My face hurt from smiling so hard.

She stretched onto her tiptoes and kissed my cheek. "Then maybe it's me who won't go away."

CHAPTER SEVENTEEN

PEPPER

I CAN'T BELIEVE *I just said that.*

For most people, it was probably a small admission. One that took no courage. But after all but admitting I like having Teague around, and I couldn't stay away either, my hands trembled slightly.

Whenever he got off work, he always came straight to the rescue . . . like it was an automatic reaction. He seemed to need us. Not in some clingy, weird way. I couldn't really explain it.

I wanted him to have a safe place. And I was happy that we seemed to fill that need.

"I know we haven't gone about this the normal way." He rubbed the side of his neck. "Hell, I still haven't taken you out on a date."

"This is a date."

He dropped his hand to his side, and all his uncertainty disappeared. "Yeah. It is."

"So that means we've been out on quite a few."

He seemed to catch on to my logic. "I like the way you think."

"Later, we could go wash all the tires on the block," I suggested, barely keeping a straight face.

"That's the perfect date." His grin was blinding in the early morning light.

"I can't do conventional." I waved back toward the rescue. It wasn't just the dogs. Whether she liked it or not, I was responsible for Miss Adeline. And sure, I could leave her to go for dinner. She'd love it if I spent the night out.

But we were a package deal.

It would take a special person to understand and accept that.

"I'm more of a rule breaker myself." Teague slid an arm around my waist and pulled me closer.

Sadie looked back at us, and I swore she rolled her eyes.

"You really want to be part of this chaos?" I stared up at him, my heart pounding.

He hovered his lips above mine. "I already am."

His mouth was warm when it landed on mine. Everything melted away, including the pent-up stress of the past few weeks.

Miss Adeline was right. Things were always fine.

I shouldn't have doubted that.

A big paw landed on my side.

Teague and I broke apart. Muffy panted as he looked back and forth between us. He had a paw on each of us.

"Yo. I'm trying to be smooth here," Teague said, scratching Muffy's head.

I bit my lip. "Not you too."

"What?"

"Yo."

He groaned. "I haven't seen Burke in a day and he's got me saying that blasted word."

"It's contagious."

Sadie tugged us toward the rescue. Apparently, she'd had enough.

Teague laced his fingers in mine. It was natural and felt right. For once, I didn't mind the cold.

We strolled to the back door. I was already exhausted, and he had to be too. Yet the burden didn't feel so heavy. In this moment, there was peace—except Sadie pawing on the metal door. But even that was a slice of normal in a time where everything was upside down.

I hadn't realized that in a lot of ways I was like the dogs, especially when it came to routine. Our days might not always be exactly the same, but there were some things that I could count on. One of them being our mealtime schedule.

Teague hadn't disrupted it. He'd slid right in seamlessly.

In a way, that was terrifying.

"You coming?" He held open the door.

The dogs were already inside, watching me stand frozen outside.

"You finally asked her to go steady?" Miss Adeline leaned against the counter, arms over her chest. "Took you long enough," she grumbled.

"I've been told I'm slow," he volleyed back good-naturedly.

"At least you got around to it." She looked at our joined hands as the door closed behind me.

It was a little weird to be affectionate with an audience, even though I could share anything and be myself with Miss Adeline. She understood what a big deal this was for me . . . maybe more than I did.

Teague yawned.

In the light, the tired lines around his eyes were more prominent. He looked like he'd been up for days.

"You should get some sleep," I said quietly.

"Do I look that bad?"

"You look like you've been hit by a truck six times," Miss Adeline volunteered.

"Not five? Or seven?" Teague asked as he loosened the leash from Ash's neck. She trotted to her kennel, took a drink of water, and lay down at Teague's feet.

"I said six, didn't I?"

"Yeah, but I'm just curious why," he said patiently.

"When you're my age, you don't have to have a reason. Six was just the first number I thought of," she huffed. "At least I didn't say six hundred."

"That's true." Teague laughed, then yawned again. "Mind if I borrow your bed?"

"Of course she doesn't."

Leave it to Miss Adeline to answer for me. I wondered why he didn't want to go home or to Lincoln's but didn't ask. Something about him wanting to be here with me made me—us—happy.

He waited for me to answer, and I liked that too.

"Not at all."

"Tuck me in?"

How was I supposed to say no to that? I nodded as Miss Adeline opened her mouth to answer for me again, the meddlesome old woman.

"You should do more than tuck him in," she offered.

I closed my eyes as my face burned.

"We're doing this at our pace." Teague's deep voice was confident as it got closer to my ear. "Our way."

I released a long breath as I opened my eyes to face him. "You know that includes direction from that one."

I pointed at Miss Adeline, who looked proud of herself, although I had no idea why. With her, I never could tell.

"I could use some advice."

I groaned. "You have no idea what you've just opened yourself up to."

"I'm willing to find out."

CHAPTER EIGHTEEN

TEAGUE

"STAY WITH ME. FOR A MINUTE."

I sounded like a child but couldn't find it in me to care. I needed Pepper close. When she was around, I forgot about all the other problems in our lives.

She blinked at me as I shrugged off my suit jacket. I needed this monkey suit off now. It was another reminder of the puppet I'd become for my father. He said wear a suit to work, so I had.

"Okay," she said so softly I barely heard her.

More of my tension melted away. I sent her a silent thank you when she slipped off her shoes.

I emptied my pockets on her dresser. Pepper's space wasn't immaculate, but it was tidy. Lived in. A loved space. A home.

"Are you going to South Carolina to pick up new dogs?" I motioned to the overnight envelope on the dresser.

She stiffened. "No."

She had a life I knew nothing about. One I was curious to connect the pieces to see what made her the person she was. While I wanted all of them now, demanding answers wasn't going to get me anywhere.

Tentatively, she walked toward me. As if whatever was in that envelope was dangerous and needed to be opened by a bomb squad.

She refused to look or touch it. Her swallow was audible when she stopped in front of me.

"It's from my hometown." She cleared her throat. "From a lawyer in my hometown," she corrected.

I bristled at the word lawyer despite that contact by one could mean anything . . . though it was probably nothing good.

"Are you—" I didn't want to assume or offend her as I tried to choose my words carefully. "In trouble?"

She half-heartedly shrugged, and her shoulders slumped even more than usual. "I haven't opened the envelope."

I nodded. It was weird how the contents of a simple envelope could hold such power.

"I got a letter from my mother on my twenty-third birthday," I blurted. The day it arrived had been routine enough. I'd been sorting through the mail like usual. When that letter was on top and the handwriting and return address registered, it nearly sent me to my knees.

"I thought she passed away when you were young?" Pepper asked, her brow furrowed.

"She did." I loosened the top few buttons of my dress shirt. My tie was in the truck somewhere. "But she wrote a bunch of letters to the three of us. I still get them at random times."

"Was she sick before she passed away?" She tilted her head.

"Not that I know of. She was just—" I paused to think how to phrase my thoughts. My mother was a special person. A bright spot to anyone who met her. She managed to show my father had a heart—at least at some point. "Thoughtful. Intuitive. And unique. The letters are so very her."

They were a gift I treasured. The randomness of the delivery dates somehow made me look forward to them even more . . . if that were possible. Mom had been there for us all these years even though she was gone.

I didn't know if she'd have given us the letters at the same times if she'd been alive, but the randomness felt calculated. How she'd known the moments that we'd need her had always baffled me. But it never failed I'd get one when I needed it.

Now would be a good time.

I knit my brow.

"What is it?"

"I wonder if she had them sent to my father too?" How would he feel if he received one? I didn't know him well enough to figure out if he'd be stoic or angry or as happy to have a piece of her as I was.

They'd loved each other. That much I remembered. She'd been gone so long it was hard to remember the glimpses of the man he was before she died. I imagined if any part of that man still existed then those letters would be as precious to him as they were to me.

And that meant we had something in common.

I could hardly bear the thought.

Pepper's expression was helpless, like she wished she had the answers but was no closer to them than I was.

She glanced toward the envelope on the dresser. "I'm scared to open it."

While I'd gathered that, her admission felt big. Like she trusted me enough to share what was going on inside her head. That was something she didn't give easily, and I'd take every crumb she was willing to offer.

"What's it going to change?"

She'd been homeless. She'd been in New York with Miss Adeline for twelve years. And that was pretty much the extent of what I knew about her past. Why had she never looked back at what she'd left behind? Or had she?

"I'm not sure. That's why I don't want to know what's inside." She fiddled with one of the clasps of her overalls.

Sadie inched closer to the edge of the bed, though she didn't get up. Her way of asking if Pepper was okay.

"Sometimes not knowing is worse than facing it."

She sighed. "It's from a lawyer. I haven't done anything wrong, but my mind automatically goes to the worst."

I wanted to reach out to her, pull her close, and promise everything would be okay. One day I would. But only when I was certain it was the truth.

"Is there anything an attorney would need to reach you for?" It was a loaded question. A nosy one. Even as I spoke it, I realized whatever the answer was, it didn't matter.

"Not that I know of," she said quietly. Her throat worked when she swallowed. "I didn't mean to end up—living at the dog track."

Something tugged in me that she couldn't say *homeless*. As if it were still too hard to admit even though she'd lived it.

I was at a loss for words. Of course she hadn't meant to end up there. What led to it?

She sat on the edge of the bed and reached for Sadie.

"I had a scholarship to a nearby college. When I graduated, it was hard to find a job. Everywhere I applied wanted someone with experience. But I couldn't get experience because no one would hire me." Her frustration was palpable and as fresh as it had been all those years ago.

"A vicious cycle," I said wryly.

Her gaze lifted to mine. "Yes."

My mind automatically went in a thousand directions. Had she wound up in her position because she couldn't find work? Did she have no one to help her? And what was wrong with all those people who wouldn't hire her? They'd made a drastic mistake.

"I ended up as a stocker at the local grocery store." She snorted bitterly. "I had all these grand illusions that I'd graduate from college and have my pick of jobs. At least I didn't go into debt for that degree."

"There was no way for you to know how difficult it would be to find work."

"I should've, considering I never intended to leave Cope and it's so small if you blink you'll miss it." She shook her head. "Looking back, it's so easy to see my mistakes."

"Did your family have a business?" I was prying again, but I wanted to hear her version of what made up the past, instead of the pieced together reality I'd formed in my mind.

"My aunt farmed on what few acres she had. She tried to tell me going to school was a waste."

What kind of person discouraged another's dreams?

One like my father.

Dread filled me. I prayed Pepper's aunt was nothing like him.

"I wanted to stand on my own," she whispered. "I wanted to prove to myself I could do it."

We had so much more in common than I'd realized. Something in me was desperate to survive without the shadow of my family name and all that money. I never wanted anyone to say I'd gotten where I was because of those things. Even though I had a safety net, very few knew about it. When I'd worked at the fire station, I'd made sure no one did. I needed to be one of the guys who understood exactly what those around me were going through. I needed to see if I would sink or swim when left to my own devices.

"And you have. Look at where you are now."

She shook her head so hard, strands of her hair came loose from her ponytail. "No. Miss Adeline has supported me all this time. I've never contributed anything but my time."

"Dedication. Hard work. Heart. Maybe what Miss Adeline needed from you wasn't money." I hated she felt she'd brought no value to their relationship when it was obvious how much she had.

"I saved what little I had," she choked out. "And I let someone steal it from me."

CHAPTER NINETEEN

PEPPER

FOR YEARS, I refused to think about any of my past.

Now the memories were on top of me like an avalanche.

The sympathy on Teague's face was almost too much to bear. Knowing where he'd come from, he couldn't understand what life had been like. Cope was about the size of this block. People survived there. They had for generations. And I'd been naïve enough to think a little bit of money was all I needed to live well.

Even before I'd been homeless, I'd never craved much. I had my backpack, a blanket my grandmother made, and a notebook with my plan for how I was going to take the small farm and make it better.

A simple life was enough for me.

Teague's sympathetic expression turned hard. "Then it seems like this letter from a lawyer should be going in an opposite direction."

Embarrassment tingled at the base of my spine. No matter how many years separated me from the past, that feeling was as fresh as it was back then. I imagined for most people anger would be the dominant emotion, but I'd always blamed myself for what happened.

I hung my head. "I started saving when I was a little girl in a box that belonged to my father." That box had been in my life from my earliest memories. It was always there.

I rubbed my thighs as my shame grew more prominent. "Every nickel I got from the time I can remember, I put in there."

It started out with mostly coins. Eventually the dark bottom was covered. And by the time I went to college, it was stuffed to the brim with ones and fives and tens and an occasional twenty.

"It was my emergency fund," I said quietly. My aunt and I had always gotten by with what little we had. As I grew older, I began to understand that things could and would go wrong. Our refrigerator went out when I was twelve. We couldn't fix it. Our neighbor couldn't fix it. And we couldn't afford even a used one.

I hated the uncertainty. And I'd promised myself that I'd never worry about money. I didn't want to be rich. Just comfortable.

Teague stayed next to the dresser like he was giving me the space he thought I needed. I appreciated that he let me talk when I was ready and didn't bombard me with a million questions. These were memories I'd just assumed stay buried.

"By the end of college, I had a little over ten thousand dollars saved." I could still remember the feel of the dark wood under my fingers when I opened it every night. The smell of the old bills hit me as if they were really in front of me again.

"Before college, I'd done odd-and-end things for the people around town, but the amount grew faster once I got a job at a barbecue restaurant in college." I paused, drawn back to the past. "It's funny when I look back on it now, but I used to count the money every day. Eventually, I forced myself to only do it once a month on the last day before I went to bed. Owning something, even something so small, meant so much to me."

I didn't know how to articulate what life had been like to Teague. If he went to Cope, he'd probably be as shell-shocked as I was the first time I set foot in New York City.

"I was quiet, especially around people I didn't know, and pretty awkward too." I looked down at my mismatched clothes and realized I probably was still awkward. I just had enough love and support that I hardly ever felt that way anymore.

Teague appeared like he wanted to object, or maybe he wanted to take up for me, but he kept his mouth closed.

"I met a guy in my last semester of college."

A scowl came from his direction.

"He'd come by the restaurant. And he was nice to me. Didn't treat me like I was invisible." I'd never had much of the good kind of attention. I preferred to be a shadow; people forgot I was around. Then they couldn't say and do hurtful things.

Teague's expression turned so hard, I wasn't sure I should keep talking. But I'd started and the words seemed to want to come out.

"We went to a few parties, but I wouldn't call it dating." I shrugged. "I guess it wasn't really friendship either." I realized how that sounded and scrambled to explain. "We weren't intimate," I said quickly as my face flamed.

He balled his fist and ate up the short distance between the dresser and the bed. The bed dipped when he sat beside me. He twined his fingers with mine.

Something about his warm hand on mine made me feel safe. *He* made me feel safe.

"Anyway, after college, he showed up in Cope." We'd talked on the phone a few times, but I'd been stunned to see him in the grocery store. "He sweet-talked my aunt into staying with us for a while. Said he wanted to buy a few acres to start a farm but his parents wouldn't support him."

Teague tightened his grip on me.

"He even took me out to see it. There was no for sale sign on it, but I didn't know how things worked." I squeezed back hard as a fresh wave of shame washed over me. "He'd ask me for five bucks, twenty bucks, fifty bucks here and there. He said his parents had cut him off and promised he was looking for work. I found him a job at a neighbor's place come harvest, but he didn't show up."

I'd never connected why he wanted a farm when he had no interest in farming. And he was from Charleston, so I didn't think he had any experience in it either.

"But he was charming. He brought something new to our dull lives." It seemed silly looking back, like I'd been chasing a shiny object.

"I loaned him the money because I understood what it was like to struggle." Even though I'd been saving all that time and hardly ever spent any of it, I wasn't stingy. If someone needed help, I wanted to do it.

"WHATCHA GOT THERE?"

I snapped the lid on my box closed and clutched it. "This was my dad's."

Curtis leaned in the doorway. "You never knew him, right?"

I shook my head. "No."

The only thing I'd known of either of my parents was the pictures of them hanging on the wall downstairs. And this box.

"At least you have a piece of him," Curtis said kindly. "Bet you keep your special stuff in it."

I shrugged. My aunt didn't even know how much I had saved in there. "Not really."

"Oh come on. What is it? A diary?" He flashed that easy grin as he stepped closer.

"No." I held the box tighter.

"Mm-hmm," he said as if he didn't believe me.

Closer. Closer. Closer he came. I resisted the urge to put the box behind me. He reached out. Everything in me seized.

Don't touch it.

He scruffed my hair. "Sweet dreams."

I didn't exhale until he left the room. Thank goodness he'd easily given up on finding out what was in my box. When I heard his door click shut down the hall, I closed my own and buried it in my closet underneath a pile of stuff.

I took a deep breath and breathed out again.

It's safe.

"PEPPER?"

I blinked at Teague, confused by the tangling of the past and present.

"Sorry. Was just seeing that time again in my head. Anyway, he disappeared one day," I whispered. "Along with my box of money."

I slumped my shoulders and leaned against his. "The whole town laughed at me when he left. They didn't know what he'd taken. But they called me a fool for thinking anyone would stick around for me. When I got my next paycheck, I packed my backpack and left town."

Teague shifted so his back was against the headboard. He pulled me between his legs and cocooned me.

"My car broke down in Virginia. I couldn't pay to fix it, so I sold it and stayed in a motel for a while. But I couldn't get a job either. I was a college graduate who couldn't manage to scrape by. It wasn't supposed to be like that." I'd studied hard to get a leg up. I'd saved so much to make sure it wasn't going to be like that. Lost. Poor. But trust in the wrong person, unwise faith in humankind, had changed the way I saw life. Again.

Teague's arms were like a safe barrier between me and the world. Inside them everything was going to be okay.

"What about your aunt? She didn't try to get you to stay?"

He'd hardly asked any questions the entire time I'd dumped it all on him. But this one . . . it still hurt. A lot.

"She blamed me for him leaving. He'd convinced her he was something he wasn't." I sighed. "I guess he'd convinced me of that too. I—I thought about if we might be something more. But I never really let myself believe that he was interested in anything like that."

I was only human. One who never had a boyfriend. Not once had I ever felt incomplete because of it. I was always busy focusing on work or school or just trying to get by. Being invisible.

I'd learned my lesson the hard way about what attention could get me.

Teague turned my face so he could look at me.

"It wasn't your fault," he said with conviction. "I know you know that. You don't need me to tell you. But I wanted you to hear it from someone who cares a whole lot about you."

The sincerity etched in every line of his features would have been enough to weaken my knees had I been standing. I felt the power of his words. I felt so many things I'd never experienced before. They were a tumbled torrent inside of me.

I didn't know how to explain any of it except that I was grateful he'd come into my life, even if it hadn't been easy from the beginning.

How did I properly thank him for being there? For sticking it out through the chaos. How did I tell him how much it meant to me that he'd listened?

Somehow I'd found the words to share part of my past, yet those two simple ones were stuck in my throat.

Since they wouldn't come, I did the only thing I knew how. The dogs had taught me how to show affection since they couldn't speak.

I crawled beside him, turned on my side, wrapped my arm over his middle, and tucked my head against his chest. His heart thumped under my ear.

Teague held me tightly and kissed the top of my head before his breathing evened out.

He understood our way of showing we cared after all.

CHAPTER TWENTY

TEAGUE

"ARE you going to open that envelope this century?"

I paused midway down the stairs, curious how Pepper would answer.

She didn't say anything right away.

"How long are you going to stand there pretending like you're not snooping?" Miss Adeline's aged face peered around the corner.

Did the woman have sonic hearing?

"You weren't as quiet as you thought," she said.

"You'll have to teach me how to sneak up on someone." I jogged down the rest of the steps.

Pepper was surrounded by dogs as she threw balls and stuffed owls and alligators from the bin of toys beside her. They raced to retrieve. Soon the box was empty and no one wanted to give up what they'd fetched. Apparently tug-of-war was the game they wanted to play.

She obliged even though she didn't have enough hands. Her easy and natural way with the dogs amazed me yet again. This was what she was meant to be doing.

"I need to go to the Elliotts' to check on our other friends," she said to one of them who refused to give up an alligator.

"Keep procrastinating," Miss Adeline muttered.

"How do you know I haven't opened it already?" Pepper asked, the question loaded with accusation.

"Because it's still sitting on the dresser unopened."

At least the woman didn't deny she was a snoop.

"You're nosy and meddlesome and—"

"Don't say something you can't take back."

"I'm not," Pepper said quickly. There was no bite to her words, just the usual volley between these two. "Meddlesome is your middle name."

"I get no respect around here." Miss Adeline looked at me and threw up her hands.

"Anybody hungry?" I asked, pretty sure I didn't want to get into the middle of this one.

"Are you cooking?" Miss Adeline asked.

"Sure." It would be nice to do something familiar.

"Don't bother going back upstairs to scrounge around to see what we've got that you can whip up," she said. "Unless Corn Flakes is on the menu."

I snorted. "I think we can do better than that."

"I have an idea." Pepper wrestled away the alligator.

"I'll take requests," I said. Learning the food she liked was another piece to her I couldn't wait to get my hands on.

"This one is for the nosy woman." She pointed at Miss Adeline. "You tell me what you offered Teague's father and I'll open the envelope."

Whoa. Pepper played hardball when she had to. And she must really want to know since I'd seen just how much she *didn't* want to open the letter.

Miss Adeline glanced back and forth between us. "It's irrelevant. Now what's for lunch?"

Pepper nodded smugly, like she knew Miss Adeline wouldn't cave. They had an interesting dynamic. In some ways, they danced around lines with one another, while in others they crossed them without abandon.

Neither of them seemed testy about pushing one another. That seemed to come from the mutual respect and love that permeated everything between them.

"I'd check to see what I have at my place, but I already know the answer." I formed my hands in the shape of a zero. "Nothing."

"Are you right on the other side of that wall?" Miss Adeline pointed in the direction of my loft . . . that I rarely went to.

"Yes ma'am."

"You any good at demolition?"

I thought we were talking about lunch?

"Umm—"

"You can't knock down walls between properties you don't own," Pepper said, like she could read the woman's mind.

I shook my finger at Miss Adeline. "I like the way you think."

Pepper groaned. "Don't encourage her."

"The same person might own both buildings," Miss Adeline said with disgust.

Pepper stopped tugging on a rope, and the dog who got it nudged her in the hand, not ready to stop their game. "What do you mean?" she asked carefully.

Miss Adeline waved her hand dismissively. "Not a thing."

Pepper narrowed her eyes. "Woman . . ."

"I thought you had too much to do to worry about me." She ambled toward the back room. "Are we taking all this group to see their friends?"

Pepper opened her mouth like she wanted to argue, but nothing came out.

Ding.

They looked at me when my phone chimed with a text.

You're late.

In my mind I thought a thousand curses. It was impossible to be late to a job when I'd never been told the hours. My father must really be enjoying himself if he took the time to text me personally.

"Everything okay?" Pepper's concerned gaze met mine.

"Just trying to decide how far I can push the boundary." I hated being at his mercy. But if I didn't show up at his command, what would he do to Pepper?

"I live to push boundaries," Miss Adeline said. "Actually I live to breathe, but you know what I meant."

"I thought you lived for the firefighter calendar." Pepper snickered.

"I forgot about that." Miss Adeline put a hand to her forehead. "It's happening. I'm going senile."

"You already were," Pepper volunteered, which earned her a warning look.

"Ladies, I've been summoned." I'd much rather stick around them today, but I'd been backed into a corner that I had every intention of getting out of. "Raincheck on the meal."

"Our rainchecks are adding up," Miss Adeline huffed, though there was admiration in her eyes. She knew why I was doing this, and I appreciated her respect.

"I thought you were going to talk to someone today about getting your old job back," Pepper said quietly.

"I can multitask. And maybe I should get my brother on that. I'm going to need a powerful attorney." I hated to ask Lincoln for one more thing, but what other choice did I have?

"Call that one with the funny last name," Miss Adeline said.

I flitted through all the lawyer commercials I'd seen on television and couldn't think of a single one with a strange name.

"You mean Zegas."

We all turned at the sound of Daniel Elliott's voice. A few dogs rushed him, Millie even attempted to go through his legs.

"That's the one," Miss Adeline said.

I'd never heard of him. Then again, I'd never had much use for lawyers.

"You could try Patrick Whitley. He's never lost a case," Vivian said from beside her husband.

Daniel flared his eyes. "Don't let Zegas hear you say that or he'll charge me double."

"Use both of them if you want a dream team." Vivian shrugged then grinned mischievously. "I'm sure they'd just *love* to work together."

"If they're the best, take them up on it," Pepper said from the floor. "I'll chip in if they're expensive."

A fist squeezed around my heart. Now I knew just how much faith she had in me by saying those words. She'd given before and had been taken advantage of. Her trust in me was something I never wanted to violate.

I nodded in silent thanks, not wanting to bring attention to just how big what she'd said was in front of other people.

"Makes a lot of sense to spend a fortune on a fancy lawyer for a fifty thousand dollar a year job, right?" I scratched my temple, pretending to mull it over.

"You lost your job?" Daniel asked, offended on my behalf.

All this support from people who weren't my siblings meant a lot to me.

"I did."

"Does Lincoln know?" Daniel reached in his pocket. Was he going to call my brother?

Another chime sounded from my hand. I didn't bother to look to see who it was.

"I better take off." I didn't want to leave, but I'd pushed my father as much as I was willing to risk . . . for now.

Pepper pushed to her feet. The dogs followed her as she took a few steps toward me. I met her halfway and opened my arms. She came into them easily. Her warmth made the difficult hours ahead easier to face.

I kissed the top of her head.

She hugged me hard before she pulled back. "I'm holding you to that raincheck."

"I'll come by whenever I finish up." Based on my pattern of behavior, I probably didn't need to say that.

"Take Me Home" played. I let it go to voicemail, not ready to release Pepper yet. Especially when I was fairly certain it was my father. The song paused for only a second before it began again.

Reluctantly I dropped one arm and checked the caller ID.

Burke.

"Yo," I answered, and Pepper smirked.

"Yo." He didn't seem to notice I'd picked up his term. "The barrels with them bodies at the park?"

I stiffened. Thinking about the fire at Pepper's park was still hard. Those barrels made it more difficult.

"Yeah?"

He didn't say anything for so long I thought we'd been disconnected.

"Burke?"

"They have a suspect."

CHAPTER TWENTY-ONE

PEPPER

"WHO IS IT?"

There was a hard edge to Teague's voice usually only reserved for his father. Certainly not Logan Burke.

I dug my nails into his arm. Ash sat up. The room was still and quiet.

He grunted at whatever response he got. "Keep me posted." Before I could ask what was going on, he touched my cheek. "They have a suspect in the park fire. Burke doesn't know who yet, but maybe some form of justice will be done."

Teague didn't seem convinced though.

What justice could those people have? They died. There was no coming back from that.

The park might never be the same, but it could be rebuilt. A second chance was possible.

For the people, they'd never have that.

Anger and sorrow swirled through me. One sick act had destroyed so much.

"Do they know who the people were?"

Did they have families? Was there someone out there still looking for them? Still hoping?

"He didn't say."

I pressed up on my toes and brushed my lips across his. I could see that Teague was frustrated but needed to get to work. I so hated that he had to work for his horrible father. "I'll see you later."

He seemed hesitant to leave yet resigned to do what was necessary. With a hug for Miss Adeline and Vivian, then a fist bump for Daniel, he disappeared out the back door.

"We were going to come see you this afternoon," I said, dusting my hands down my overalls.

"Beat you to it." Vivian almost skipped over and flopped down on the desk. Millie nosed between her legs and got exactly what she wanted: a head scratch. "And turns out we're dog people. Who knew?"

"If you weren't, we wouldn't like you," Miss Adeline said.

I bit my lip so as not to laugh. She wasn't lying.

"We have a proposition for you."

Vivian snickered, and Daniel's face turned red. I had a suspicion not many people had the ability to do that to him.

"What he's trying to say is we have an idea." His wife attempted to bail him out.

I glanced at Miss Adeline to gauge if she had any clue about what-ever they were up to. She appeared as caught off guard as I was.

He scowled. Then again, he always did.

"We've acquired our building." He bent to pet Muffy, seeming more comfortable around the dogs than he had been when we'd dropped the others off at their home.

And the whole building? I couldn't begin to compute how much that must have cost. Plus, they seemed to have money left over.

It was mind-boggling.

"The bottom floor had a fitness area and some meeting rooms and some other stuff." Vivian twirled her finger in a whoop-de-do motion. "In all the time I've lived there, I'd never checked any of it out."

"Why would you when we have everything we need upstairs?" Daniel asked innocently.

They probably did have a fitness room and whatever else in that ginormous apartment. And it didn't even matter to them. I bet if we wanted to use it, we wouldn't have to ask.

"*Anyway.*" Vivian rolled her eyes, though the two of them seemed to be in sync as they laid out their plans. "We're slowly renovating as our family moves in and hadn't really decided what we want to do with other parts of the building."

"We won't be needing the community amenities any longer." Daniel finally joined his wife by the desk.

Miss Adeline was suspiciously quiet as she listened.

"We'd like to have a second location of Grey Paws downstairs." Vivian beamed when the grand plan finally came out.

I looked at Miss Adeline, who was as wide-eyed as I felt. We had more than we could do here. And while I appreciated their generosity, we couldn't stretch ourselves any further with a second location. Not without help.

Although, at the moment we *were* operating in two locations.

"We've attracted a lot of attention walking the dogs," Vivian said. "In fact, we have the phone numbers of a few potential adopters. And a partnership with Paths of Purpose would be a fantastic program."

I hadn't had time to go speak to the woman who runs the facility. That should move up the to-do list because I agreed. The dogs and the residents could benefit greatly from one another.

In my head, I couldn't figure out the logistics of the program. Who would oversee it? Would the dogs come back to the rescue every evening? How could we run that when we barely had time to do what was needed here?

"We've overwhelmed you." Uncertainty formed on Vivian's face.

"With your generosity," Miss Adeline finally said.

"But you hate the idea." Vivian frowned.

"No," I said quickly. "This is a lot to consider. And to be honest, we barely have time to think."

How tired I was hit me out of nowhere. But it didn't matter how I felt. These dogs needed me.

"You were planning to go over this afternoon to check on the dogs. Why don't you take a look at the space?"

My brows furrowed. Miss Adeline had built this home and this dream with the love of her life. She'd never talked of expanding. There was something in her tone I didn't like.

Daniel and Vivian were kind enough to make the offer. They'd obviously put a lot of thought into the idea.

"I'd love to. Can you hold things together for a little while until I get back?" I tilted my head.

Miss Adeline wrinkled her nose. "I've been holding this place together since it started."

She most definitely had.

"Are you free now?" I looked at Daniel and Vivian.

"Sure." Vivian clapped her hands happily. "Want to take these guys to see their friends?"

Sadie eyed me from where she was pretending to sleep on the floor with a *don't make me move* look.

"Maybe another time."

As if she could understand human speak, Sadie closed her eyes again, able to relax.

"Unless you want to come too?" I asked.

Miss Adeline was crucial to every element of this rescue. She should be part of any potential expansion. She'd see things in the new space that I couldn't.

Sadie glared at me. It was impossible but I swore she did.

"Nah. That means I'd have to go out in the cold."

I studied her for a second to make sure she was okay with staying behind. The last thing I wanted was for her to feel left out. "We can video chat when we get there."

She nodded.

Vivian grabbed my hand and pulled me toward the door. "We've already donated the exercise equipment. That room is so huge. But it has mirrors. Will the dogs be okay with that?"

I struggled to keep up as she spoke in rapid-fire, but I appreciated her enthusiasm.

"Oh, and I hope you're okay with taking the subway," she said.

My brain ping-ponged as she went from one subject to another.

"Give her a minute to get it all out before you answer," Daniel said affectionately.

She punched him in the arm. "Don't worry. We'll behave on the tour . . . maybe."

Somehow I doubted they would.

CHAPTER TWENTY-TWO

TEAGUE

"THANKS FOR COMING BY."

Burke glanced toward the fire station. It was dark out, not to mention cold. The lights were on, and it was weird not being able to go inside.

A pang of longing landed square in my chest.

His earlier call had bothered me all afternoon. Then when I'd gotten the text asking me to drop by the station, I'd been anxious to see what was going on.

"It's weird being here," I admitted before I thought better of it.

He grimaced. "It ain't the same without your sorry ass around."

"That your way of saying you miss me?" I leaned on my truck and folded my arms.

"Not a chance." He shot me the bird. Had I picked that up from him too?

"I won't tell anyone." I cupped my hands around my mouth like I was about to shout it out.

He yanked on my arms, and I laughed.

That earned me another middle finger.

He leaned against the truck beside me. "How you holding up?"

When anyone got fired, it was difficult. I didn't want to put firemen up on a pedestal, but it was different than a lot of other professions. I hadn't just lost a fifteen-year career, I'd lost my brothers.

Yeah, I could still see them, but it wasn't the same as working side by side.

"I'm hanging in there. Hasn't really set in yet."

Plus I have a stellar new career waiting for me.

Burke made a noncommittal noise. This was a subject we all wanted to avoid.

"I didn't want to say anything on the phone." He spoke in a hushed tone despite no one was around.

Did he know who the suspect was in the fire?

"Ellen had an autopsy done."

I jerked my head toward him. "Why did she do that?"

Cassano, who had been my partner for five years, died from injuries related to the fire. One minute I thought he'd been improving, but the next, he was dead. A heart attack. But now, with the autopsy being requested, I couldn't help the darker thoughts. Murder. I should have been able to save him. I hadn't collapsed the floor, but I still felt responsible. And yet . . . had I been blaming myself for no reason? Was that what Burke was suggesting?

"Said a man his age shouldn't have died from a heart attack."

She'd been so broken up at the funeral, as we all were; I couldn't believe she'd had the thought to have an autopsy performed. It hadn't occurred to me. I couldn't imagine what she felt like losing her husband.

"Does she have the results?" I asked carefully, not sure I wanted to hear them.

"Not yet. I just talked to her this morning." He leaned closer and looked around again. "You know I've got a friend on the investigation unit."

"Yeah?" If this weren't such a serious conversation, I'd ask him why he didn't try to get transferred over there. He loved trying to connect dots at the scenes.

"Remember there were two dead people at that fire?"

Marshmallows. *Ugh.* I shouldn't have thought that. But the whole department had rubbed off on me.

I pressed my temples. "What does that have to do with Cassano?"

Burke glanced around one more time. "Both of them died of heart attacks."

His eyes were round like he'd just dropped the mic. I couldn't believe there was enough left of either of them to be able to tell what had caused their deaths . . . other than the obvious smoke inhalation.

"I was there, Burke. No heart issues." I pointed to my chest.

He hit me with the back of his hand. "Maybe Cassano saw something when you were in there. Something that could've implicated the killer."

"We were together the whole time. Besides, we couldn't see a damn thing in that place." I respected Burke and his instincts, but he was grasping at connections that simply weren't there.

"That ain't all," he said, sounding offended.

I held up both hands in surrender. "I'm not blowing off your idea. Just trying to keep a level head about it."

"One of them bodies in the barrel. Give you one guess what they died of." He held up his finger in a number one gesture.

"Heart attack."

He nodded smugly. "No such thing as coincidences."

I looked down at my feet as I absorbed everything he'd just told me. "It's weird. I'll give you that."

"Damn straight it's weird. It's connected. Has to be."

"Whoa. Let's not get ahead of ourselves." The fires were arson. No doubt about that. Were we dealing with a serial arsonist? Or just an odd set of similar circumstances?

"Any proof that the two fires were started in the same manner?" I asked. Most of the time, arsonists who set multiple fires had a ritual. There was a method to the apparent madness.

Burke's face crumpled. "I don't know." He was more aware of the pattern of behavior of people who set fires because he enjoyed studying them.

"And if Cassano is connected, his death was an abnormality. There was no fire after his heart attack. It was before." It was a piece that didn't fit . . . *if* these pieces went together at all.

"There's got to be a reason," he said with determination. "I'm gonna check all the fires with deaths in the past few months. See if there's something we missed before."

"If Captain catches you snooping around this . . ." Our job was to fight fires. And gossip—the who, what, when, where, and why—was the investigation unit's territory. At least it had been since Captain had taken over.

"What he doesn't know can't hurt him," he huffed. "Besides, I never understood what the big deal was about finding out what happens at the fires we fight. Sometimes they stick with you."

They did. Even when I compartmentalized. And these latest ones were so horrific, they were impossible to forget.

"There weren't too many deaths in the past few months," I said, and he brightened. "It shouldn't be too hard to track if there were any other heart attacks."

"You're right." His tone said he'd be calling his friend as soon as we finished talking.

"You know how easy it is for things to look like they go together when they don't. Remember those fires a few years back? They convicted an innocent man of setting sixteen fires."

His shoulders slumped. "I remember. But this is connected. I feel it."

I tossed my keys and caught them. It was like a nervous tic. I didn't like thinking about the fires being connected. If they were, that likely meant something sinister was at play.

"You really think Cassano's 'heart attack'"—I put air quotes around heart attack—"wasn't an accident?"

I struggled to get the words out. It was one thing when I blamed myself for his death, but another to think someone else could've been responsible.

"I don't know. But as soon as that tox screen is available, I'm going over every letter." He pounded on the side of my truck.

"And what if it really was a heart attack?" With all of these questions, it was like Cassano had been buried, but we couldn't begin to heal. Maybe we wouldn't anyway.

"Then it's just more proof we're not invincible. We're both older than he was."

And we could die of a heart attack too, if he could.

But Burke didn't speak that part aloud. Didn't have to. I knew exactly what he was thinking.

"Burke! Where the hell are you?" Rivera appeared under one of the lights on the fire station with his hands cupped around his mouth.

"Yo!" he called back.

"You got a secret girlfriend out here or what?" Rivera took a few steps toward us.

"Better than that."

When Rivera caught sight of me in the shadows he jogged over. "You bastard."

We slapped hands and he pulled me in for a bro hug.

"Miss me?" I flicked my chin toward the station.

"Your ugly ass? Not a chance." He smacked my shoulder.

Brrrrrrrrinngggg.

"Shit. We gotta go," Rivera said when the alarm sounded.

They raced toward the firehouse. Burke turned around and jogged backward. "I'll call you."

I jumped in my truck and jetted before Captain caught me hanging around.

When I passed by Pepper's park, I pulled into an empty spot. Could all of these fires be connected? Or was Burke's CSI imagination working overtime?

Everything was discombobulated and swirled in my head. If they were connected, how? And if there were no coincidences, then why was the latest fire in Pepper's park?

I groaned. Burke had me paranoid now.

Hopefully, he'd have the name of that suspect soon, and we could put to rest all these theories. And I prayed that was all they were.

Theories.

CHAPTER TWENTY-THREE

PEPPER

"I CAN'T OPEN IT."

I threw down the envelope from the attorney on the kitchen table.

Miss Adeline munched on her cereal. "Then don't."

I stared. My mostly untouched dinner was getting soggier by the second.

"I thought you wanted me to."

She slurped some milk from the bowl. "I'm curious, but what does it matter in the end? If that thing makes you unhappy, toss it."

She stood, grabbed the trash can, and held it out to me.

I slumped in my chair. "I can't throw it away either."

"Then open it."

I pushed my bowl away. "You're no help."

"If you need me to open it, you should've just said so in the first place." She swiped the envelope from beside me and pulled on the tab.

"Wait."

She'd torn about an inch open.

She lifted a brow in a *what do you want me to do* gesture.

I folded my arms on the table and dropped my forehead onto them. "Arghhh."

"Anybody home?"

Dogs barked and bolted to the door. Except Sadie, who barely opened her eyes.

I snapped my head up at Teague's voice.

He appeared in the doorway in a suit minus the tie. I still couldn't get used to him dressed that way.

"Did you know the back door was unlocked?" He frowned.

"No. I'm sure I secured it." I tried to think about the last time I'd taken the dogs out. "Do you mean not closed or not locked?"

"Not locked," he confirmed.

"We never unlock it," Miss Adeline said. "If we're loading or unloading the van, we prop it open with a rock."

"And that was before all the trouble started." Worry flitted through me. I *knew* I hadn't unlocked that door. I kept the key on me at all times.

"I only went out the front today." Miss Adeline seemed as concerned as I was.

In the chaos of feeding dogs and walking them, anything could happen. But that was one thing we were diligent about. Locking the back door.

"What made you try it? You usually text."

Teague glanced away. "I don't know. I just . . . did."

Why was he acting so weird?

"I guess I feel more at home here than anywhere else," he said quickly. "I—I didn't think. I just acted."

A tinge of red colored his cheeks as he met my eyes. He wasn't ashamed. Just embarrassed. I could see that. Even the littlest admissions of how someone felt could be hard. I understood that as well as anyone.

And this was beginning to feel like it was his home. When he wasn't around, there was a hole where he should've been.

"Is that your way of saying you're moving in?"

I slid farther down my chair and cut my eyes over to Miss Adeline. The woman was unafraid to say anything.

She shrugged at my incredulous look. "You won't ask, so I'll cut through the crap."

That was one way of putting it.

Teague held up the duffle bag hidden behind him. "Maybe?"

I pointed back and forth between them. "I'm going to have to watch the two of you."

"Please." Miss Adeline waved me off. "You know I'm only looking out for you."

"Me too," Teague said quietly. "And sorry about dinner. Again. Am I too late for Corn Flakes?"

"She won't let us have Lucky Charms," Miss Adeline grumbled. "Hope you like granola and fiber." She made a face.

"It's good for us." Teague grinned and threw down his bag by the counter. "I'm going to have a look around, then I'll be back."

Ash happily followed him as he disappeared.

"What do you think happened to that door?" I asked.

Miss Adeline polished off the milk in her bowl and wiped her mouth. "I have no idea."

"Daniel and Vivian came by, but I don't remember them going in the back."

"Lexie and Eric dropped off the food this afternoon." She lifted a shoulder and lowered it. "But we let them in and out."

"Maybe it happened then." It was hard to remember when so much else was happening.

"Speaking of the Elliotts, what do you think of their proposal?" She leaned back and folded her hands. "It was hard to tell on the video chat, but it looked nice."

"Believe it or not, they have more space there than we do here." The area they'd showed me earlier was overwhelming in a good way. It was easy to envision a setup for the dogs that was conducive to their wellbeing.

"Oh I believe it."

"They're even willing to knock down some walls and create an outdoor space indoors." It was hard to wrap my head around, especially when Vivian started talking fast.

I wanted that for the dogs we had now and the ones in the future.

"But?" Miss Adeline knew me too well.

"This is home. And we're already spread so thin. How can we make two locations work?" The idea of another location excited me for the dogs but stressed me out thinking about the logistics.

"At some point you're going to have to rescue less dogs or learn to give up some control." Her eyes bored into me. "To trust."

I let out a long sigh as a pit formed in my stomach. "I hate when you talk like that."

"I'm on borrowed time." She held up both hands when I opened my mouth. "Everybody at my age is."

A lump formed in my throat. "I can't do this without you."

"You're already better than I ever was. You run this place. I'm just here as the entertainment." She pouted. "I can't even say I'm the beauty of this operation anymore."

I laughed. "I know some firemen who would disagree."

She grinned. "Yeah, they would."

"Everything looks secure." Teague breezed back into the apartment like he'd always lived here.

"That's so weird." I still couldn't figure out how that door had gotten unlocked.

"I double-checked. All the doors are locked now."

"Has it been forty-eight hours?"

Dread filled me at Miss Adeline's question. I hadn't completely forgotten about the inspector, but I had managed to push him to the back of my mind.

"I think so, but the days are all running together."

"What's in forty-eight hours?" Teague rummaged through the cabinets until he found a bowl.

"The inspector is supposed to come back," I said.

He grabbed the cereal box off the counter. "I doubt he will, now that I'm working for my father."

"So that was connected?" I pushed the milk toward him as he sat.

"I don't have proof, but my guess is yes." The cereal tinkled in the ceramic bowl as he poured. "Cassano's widow, Ellen. If I could get her to come by, would you mind if she spent some time with the dogs? I think it would be a good distraction. Might make her feel better."

"Absolutely," I said, well aware of the power of healing these dogs had. They couldn't take away the loss, but they could definitely lift her spirits.

"Bet you anything, she'll fall in love with one of these mutts." Miss Adeline petted Lucky affectionately. His leg was healing nicely, even though it seemed like we'd rescued the dogs from the track in New Jersey a lifetime ago.

"Who wouldn't?"

Ash had her head resting on Teague's lap. The sweet girl wasn't even looking for crumbs. She was so attached to him.

"She can't have that one." Miss Adeline motioned toward Ash.

Teague nodded in agreement then flicked his chin at my full cereal bowl. "You'd rather have Lucky Charms?"

I held up the envelope. "Lost my appetite."

"What's in there?"

"She wouldn't know. She won't open it and won't let me, but she won't throw it away either." Miss Adeline had a way of putting things in perspective.

I closed my eyes and yanked on the pull tab. The ripping sound of the cardboard did nothing to ease my nerves.

Miss Adeline put her hand on mine. "Remember. This changes nothing."

"I know." But I wasn't so sure.

I pulled out a thick piece of paper. Only one page was inside on an attorney's letterhead.

I hesitated before I let my eyes drift down the page any farther. *Nothing changes.*

I skimmed past the salutation and only made it to the first sentence.

The paper crinkled as I clutched it with both hands.

"My aunt and my parents died." The words were yanked from my throat. "In a fire."

CHAPTER TWENTY-FOUR

TEAGUE

PEPPER SHOOK as she held the letter.

"I thought your parents were already dead," Miss Adeline said sharply.

"So did I," Pepper whispered.

I dropped my spoon and reached across the table for her hand. "I —" Sorry wasn't adequate. I didn't want to be that person who said the word to her.

The letter floated to the table. She placed her hand in mine. It trembled as I squeezed.

Miss Adeline snatched the paper, and Pepper reached for her with her free hand. I liked that she wasn't afraid to show us what she needed.

With every second that passed, Miss Adeline's face shifted from hard to angry to outrage.

"The insurance won't pay for the house because it was arson. Apparently, all three of them owe quite a bit of money, and since you're next of kin and the house was the only asset they had, that debt falls on you."

"What?" Pepper croaked. "They can't do that. I didn't even know my parents were alive. They abandoned me with my aunt." Her voice rose and then broke.

And my heart shattered for her.

How anyone could have left her was unfathomable. Hearing how much that still hurt her . . . made me want to drag them out of their graves and shake them.

"I'm not sure that's correct," I said, though I had no experience like this. When my mother passed away, everything had been set up well in advance as far as her estate went.

Miss Adeline studied the letter. "The property transfers to you since you're the only remaining relative."

"I don't want it!" Pepper pushed back from the table, severing the connection she had with us.

She rushed to the balcony doors and marched through them. Sadie lifted her head, then lazily got up to investigate. Through the windows, Pepper cradled the dog from where she sat in a rocking chair.

I was halfway out of my seat when Miss Adeline put a hand on mine.

"Give her a minute."

She needed me. I didn't want her to suffer for one second alone. Reluctantly, I sat.

Pepper's aunt had blamed her for things that weren't her fault and she'd ended up homeless as a result. Her parents' abandonment . . . I couldn't think about that or my rage would cripple me.

They'd all put her through hell while they were alive and couldn't have the decency to leave her alone in death, despite they'd damn well made it look easy when Pepper had needed them.

"Daniel texted me the names of those lawyers earlier. We may need them to fight for Pepper." I pulled out my phone, glad to be doing something, although I wished I could take it all away for her.

Miss Adeline let out a satisfied grunt. "She's gonna need more than a lawyer."

"I'll pay the debt if that's what it takes."

I had the money. I just didn't advertise it.

Her gray brow lifted. "That letter doesn't say how much it is."

"I can cover whatever amount it is." I was ninety-nine percent sure the three of them couldn't possibly have as much debt as my mother left me in a trust, but if they had, I'd hit up Lincoln and Beau. If I had to, I'd get on my knees and beg my father.

Whatever it took to help Pepper was what I'd do.

"I don't want those assholes to get a penny," she said through gritted teeth. "I have half a mind to go down to South Carolina and tell that lawyer where he can shove this letter."

I pressed my lips together. It was a totally inappropriate time to want to laugh, but the woman was a trip. I had no doubt she'd do exactly what she said, and I'd be right there with her as backup.

"Have I waited long enough?" I itched to go to Pepper. I might be able to fix this, but I needed to put my arms around her.

"I said a minute. It hasn't even been thirty seconds."

It felt like forever.

"If this backfires, I'll heed your advice next time." The chair scraped when I stood.

"Fat chance." She flicked her hand toward the balcony. "Go get her. And if you aren't coming inside anytime soon, turn on the heater out there so you don't freeze to death."

"Hang out here in case I need backup," I said as I made my way across the room.

"I hope you have her smiling before I get out of my seat. It takes me a while to get up, you know."

She actually moved pretty well for a person her age, but I didn't argue.

The cold hit me as I neared the door. Ash was on my heels, along with her pal Muffy.

Pepper was balled up in a chair, but Sadie now lay at her feet.

I took the chair beside her, though I was dissatisfied with that. It wasn't close enough for me to hold her the way I wanted to.

For a while, we sat in silence. Every time I opened my mouth to say something, I closed it. Nothing sounded right in my head, and she needed more than the typical lines people said when something bad happened.

"How'd that lawyer find me?"

In true Pepper fashion, she saved me from saying something stupid.

"I haven't talked to anyone in that town since the day I left," she continued, as if she were having a conversation with herself.

"We're all more accessible with the advances in technology." Okay. So that sounded lame.

She cut her eyes at me in obvious agreement.

"All I mean is it's not that hard if you're willing to dig," I amended quickly.

"It's like the ultimate screw you. And now none of them are around to give me any answers." She threw her hands up. Sadie lifted her head to check on Pepper. She sniffed a few times and let out a satisfied sigh.

"What would you want to know?" Maybe it was better when I kept my mouth shut. Maybe I needed Miss Adeline as backup now. She wouldn't fumble her way through this.

"Why they lied. What did I ever do to any of them?" Pepper's voice cracked, but she didn't cry.

"How they treated you says more about them than it does you." And while that was true, I still felt I wasn't doing anything to comfort her.

"I'd have rather known they didn't want me." She hugged her knees. "It would've hurt. A lot. But the truth is always better than a lie."

"You aren't going to pay their debts," I said resolutely. I didn't want her to have to give this a second thought.

"I just want it to go away. I'd moved on and now here it is again."

That I understood. Unfortunately, I didn't have an answer for how to give her what she wanted. My father was the gift that kept on giving. Her family seemed to be the same.

"You should talk to a lawyer."

"I can't afford a lawyer," she cried. Sadie barked like she was scolding me for upsetting Pepper.

"Don't worry about that," I said evenly.

"How can I not worry about it? And what if I have to pay off their debt? I make it because Miss Adeline keeps me afloat."

"Don't do that."

"Do what?"

"Belittle the value you bring to Grey Paws." I hated to hear her talk like that. She didn't realize how needed she was. That meant more than all the money in the world. If money could solve problems, my family would be happy campers.

"You don't have any idea what it's like to find out the parents you thought were dead your whole life really weren't. So don't tell me what to do," she snapped. "I have to walk the dogs."

She popped up, and I caught her hand as she passed. "I'm not trying to." Shit. "I want to fix this for you. Instead I'm making it worse. But I'm here, whatever you need me for."

She stared at me. Raw pain reflected in her dark pools. Something in me cracked at how deeply she was hurting.

I got to my feet and pulled her into my arms. To my surprise, she yielded. Her forehead dropped to my chest, and she fisted my shirt.

"I just want everything to go back to the way it was."

She hadn't meant to, but it stung.

Before Pepper, my life had routine and purpose, but it had been dull. I felt . . . empty. As if something had been missing. A Pepper-shaped hole. To go back to that would be worse than anything else I'd gone through in my life. When did she become my world? Why would I ever want to go back to that time of loneliness?

I tipped her chin up so she was forced to look at me. This beautiful and brave woman.

"I don't."

CHAPTER TWENTY-FIVE

PEPPER

I DON'T HAVE *time for this.*

Yet here I was in the elaborate lobby of the office of Kane Zegas, one of the most high-profile attorneys in the city.

"This isn't necessary," I whispered.

Teague was undeterred as he held my hand. "That SOB who sent you that letter won't know what hit him after Zegas is done with him." He squeezed my hand. "Daniel said that. Not me. And he'd know."

I appreciated how they'd all rallied around me, but I didn't like dragging the Elliotts even deeper into my problems. When it came to the dogs, there was nothing I wouldn't do, my pride be damned.

But this was personal.

And embarrassing.

I had a family who never wanted me, and yet, they expected me to pay their bills after they were dead.

They didn't have the decency to ask me for money when they were alive. Well, not since I'd left town.

There was a dull ache in my chest that hadn't gone away since I'd read that letter.

The news that my parents had been alive all this time still seemed impossible.

Where had they been? Why had they left me with my aunt? How had they stayed away?

Aunt Sally barely spoke of them. There'd been a few pictures around her house, and that was all I'd known of the two people I thought died in an accident on a lake right after I was born.

Had the whole town known they weren't really dead?

No wonder they all thought I was a fool.

Stupid Pepper was too dumb to realize her parents had abandoned her, not died. Because nobody wanted her. Not even her aunt.

Why had my aunt bothered to raise me? She didn't want me. And now I'd likely never know the answers to any of it.

They were all dead.

This time officially.

"What's running through your head?" Teague's voice was deep and soothing and not judging. His concern was in every syllable.

"A million questions." I wanted to pull my knees to my chest, but it wasn't appropriate to put my shoes on the expensive leather of the chair. "Do you think my parents were in town the whole time?"

"No. Someone would've said something to you." The sympathy on his face caused me to turn away. "People can't keep their mouths shut."

Deep down I knew he was right, though part of me wondered if the whispers behind my back had been about how I wasn't an orphan but abandoned.

"Come with me." A man in a pinstripe suit strode through the glass front entrance. He exuded confidence and power. His gray hair was peppered with streaks of black. He was strikingly handsome, probably knew it, and didn't seem to care.

When neither Teague nor I stood, he waved us over. If this was Kane Zegas, he certainly didn't seem interested in schmoozing potential clients.

We hustled down the hall through a set of double mahogany doors into an expansive office.

"I read the letter." He tossed his briefcase on his desk and collapsed in the chair behind it. "I also had a surface check of assets of the deceased."

Teague and I took the chairs in front of his desk, even though he hadn't offered them. I liked that Mr. Zegas, at least I presumed that was who this was, was so detached. If he'd referred to my family as such, it made them more human, more real. And I needed the distance.

For all practical purposes, they were strangers to me even if I shared their blood.

"They had zilch." Zegas leaned back, clearly at ease in his domain. "They were behind on everything. Utilities, property taxes, loans."

I appreciated that this man had practically no time to study the situation, yet he was familiar enough with it that he didn't even refer to any notes.

"If you have nothing, why would you go to the trouble of paying an attorney to sort out your estate?" His sharp gaze landed on me.

It was such a simple question, one that made perfect sense. I felt silly for not thinking of it earlier. In the onslaught of emotion, it hadn't occurred to me how odd it was my aunt had a lawyer.

"When is the last time you had contact with the deceased?"

"Thirteen years ago," I answered easily. "My aunt, that is. I wasn't aware my parents were alive."

He picked up a pen and made a note. "When you were in correspondence with her, were you ever aware of her retaining legal counsel?"

"No."

There'd been one lawyer in Cope. We knew who he was, but he and his family lived in the biggest house in town and pretty much didn't know people like us existed.

"Do you want the property in question?"

The man didn't waste time, and I appreciated his directness. Teague remained quiet, like he was a silent support beside me. I was so glad he was here.

"Absolutely not." I never wanted to go back to South Carolina, let alone own the property that would only remind me of my mistakes.

"I'll draft a letter rejecting the assets. If you accept them, you can be held liable for the associated debt. Since you have no interest, and you aren't legally obligated to take them, this should be fairly cut and dried." He put on a pair of reading glasses. "I've contacted a colleague of mine licensed to practice in the state of South Carolina. I'll have him cross-check in case there are any laws I'm not aware of."

"Thank you." My head spun. Was it this easy to get rid of the mess they'd left me?

"The thing you need to ask yourself is who retained that attorney. How did he know where you are? Why would they bother to involve you?" Zegas leaned forward, his gaze penetrating.

"I don't know," I whispered.

"Can you fix this?" Teague asked tightly.

Zegas flicked an annoyed glance in his direction. "I said I could."

"Sorry I'm late. New baby. No sleep."

We spun around. A younger man in an equally expensive looking suit rushed into the office.

"I don't know why Elliott thinks we need you too," Zegas muttered.

"I'm Patrick Whitley," the other man said as he dropped onto a nearby sofa. He pulled papers from his briefcase and scattered them on the coffee table.

"By all means, make yourself at home." Zegas waved his arm in the general direction of the sitting area. "I thought you weren't practicing anymore anyway."

I glanced between the two men, confused by their dynamic. Did they like each other?

"Which is why you should be grateful I'm here," Whitley said.

"Your wife is probably glad to have you out of the house."

Teague cleared his throat and stood. "How soon can you get this mess cleared up for Pepper?"

"I'll send the letter this week. From there, the time frame depends on the legal system," Zegas said.

"Thank you. We'll let you two get to your next case." I pushed to my feet.

"Aren't you the fireman who was fired?" Whitley paused, shuffling through papers.

"Yeah?" Teague gripped the back of his chair.

"That's why I'm here. Did I miss something?" Whitley grabbed a legal pad and pen.

"Pepper is most important."

I appreciated Teague putting my needs ahead of his own. He had two great lawyers at his disposal, and I wanted him to take advantage of them even if it was just to clear his good name.

"I think we're done with my issue. I'll wait in the lobby while you fill them in on yours." I reached for my purse and stood. "Mr. Zegas, I'll give your secretary contact information so you can send me a bill."

He waved me off. "I'll charge Daniel extra next time."

Somehow, I didn't think he was joking. "I'd prefer to pay my own way."

The Elliotts had done more than enough for me. I might have to cut off my right arm to pay for the precious few minutes of time Kane Zegas had given me, but I wouldn't saddle them with any more IOUs.

He opened his mouth to speak, but Teague stood and shot him a look I couldn't decipher.

Then he turned and focused those chocolate pools on me. "Stay. Please."

We both circled back to the chairs we'd just vacated.

"Oh don't be all stuffy and sit over there." Whitley motioned us over. "These chairs are more comfortable than those."

"For Christ's sake," Zegas grumbled as he rolled his chair back. "This is my office, you know. Have I no authority anymore?"

"At least you aren't gloating about how you saved my ass." Whitley looked up toward the ceiling. "Thank goodness for small mercies."

"Elliott owes me for this. It was bad enough when I had you for a client." Zegas dropped onto the opposite end of the sofa.

I glanced at Teague who looked as clueless as I felt. If Zegas hadn't immediately come up with some incredibly legitimate questions regarding my case, I'd be second-guessing that these two lawyers were the best of the best.

Teague cleared his throat. "You're not charging me for the time you bicker, right?"

Whitley burst out laughing. "He will." He pointed at Zegas. "If I were you, I'd check your bill."

CHAPTER TWENTY-SIX

TEAGUE

"WHAT DO YOU THINK?"

Ash pulled me down the sidewalk with a little harder tug than usual. Muffy had found something interesting to smell up ahead, and she was curious too.

"That I'm ready for summer so my face won't freeze off," I said.

"You just want car wash season," Pepper volleyed back.

"And you and that one still owe me." I pointed toward Muffy.

Sadie stopped to smell the end of my finger.

"She likes peanut butter and jelly," Pepper said with a hint of affectionate annoyance. "And I meant about the lawyers. What do you think of them?"

We'd come straight back to Grey Paws after our meeting and immediately began the routine of walking dogs. I hadn't really given Zegas and Whitley much thought.

"They're an odd couple, but each have their own strengths," I said carefully.

"One of them has never lost."

"That doesn't necessarily mean anything when it comes to my case." Going up against the city of New York wasn't an easy thing.

And really, when it came to any case, the previous records could be tossed out.

"He's proven. That's something. And I liked him. Both of them, actually." She tilted her head to the side as if that puzzled her.

"I did too." I adjusted the leash. "They seem undaunted to go head-to-head with the city."

"They were excited about it." Pepper tossed Muffy a treat after he did his business.

"They were."

Sadie nudged Pepper's hand.

"You haven't gone yet."

Ash squatted on a patch of grass and wagged her tail at Pepper, who promptly fed her a biscuit. Sadie stamped her feet impatiently.

"You know what you have to do," Pepper said.

Sadie pawed her pocket.

"That's not it."

Sadie pawed again.

I snickered.

"Don't encourage her." Pepper's warning look sent a chill through me.

"Sorry," I said, straightening up immediately.

Pepper grinned.

Sadie pawed so hard, she ripped the pocket of Pepper's overalls. The baggie of treats fell onto the sidewalk and Sadie gobbled them down in one swallow. She looked at Pepper as if to say "I win."

"*Sadie.*" Pepper picked up the trash and deposited it in a nearby garbage bin. "How am I supposed to get mad at her?" She looked at her torn pocket. "She's creative and persistent."

"That she is." I petted the mischievous girl's head. "She is something else."

"Let's head back so I can patch this up." The fabric dangled, exposing a peek of her thigh I tried not to notice.

We meandered toward the rescue.

"What did you think about Zegas's theory? About your aunt hiring an attorney. Especially since there's no will."

When Zegas had proposed the question, Pepper seemed like she'd been hit over the head with a two by four. It *was* a great question. One none of us had considered because we were too absorbed by the shock of the news.

"It's interesting. But if she didn't contact him and my parents didn't, then who did?" She implored me for answers with her eyes. "Who would want to load me up with all of their debt? Who benefits if I take on that debt? Miss Adeline is the only person I have consistent contact with."

I stopped. "You don't think she did it?"

"No!" Pepper halted abruptly. "I just meant I don't know anyone really. I don't have any friends, but I don't have any enemies either."

The thought of her only having one person in her life made me feel strange. At least Miss Adeline loved her and was a worthy friend. Pepper was so amazing. She should have lots of friends.

And she did have Daniel and Vivian. Even Lexie and her brother, who brought the dog food.

Pepper had more people who cared for her than she realized.

I wanted to surround her with so much love that she'd never be touched again by any ugliness.

Not that I loved her.

I took in her disheveled appearance.

I loved that her hair was always loose from her ponytail.

I loved that there were usually paw streaks on her clothes.

I loved that she had no idea how beautiful she was.

I loved how she took care of Miss Adeline.

I loved how she put the dogs above all else.

I loved that she was always there for me.

I loved that her heart was the biggest I'd ever seen even though she had every reason for it not to be.

"Teague?" A line of worry creased her forehead.

"I love you," I blurted out the terrifying words when the realization hit me.

"What?" Her arm went limp, and for a second I was afraid she was going drop the leashes in her hand.

"I love you." The statement was more confident when I repeated it. Now that I'd test-driven it on my tongue a couple of times, it felt right.

I half expected her to take Ash and leave me out on the sidewalk.

"I—" Her face was a mix of confusion and hope. "How?"

"I just do." I cupped her cheek, and she leaned into my palm. It was cold from the wind.

"I—"

Her struggle for a response made me love her even more.

"This is our spot now." I leaned in close.

There was a letterbox, some dead grass around a tree, and a shuttered business with profanity graffitied on it.

She glanced around. Grey Paws was in sight. Maybe it would've been better if I'd had my epiphany in front of it. But I couldn't control where my mind went.

"It might not be the most romantic, but I just realized I'm in love with you, so that makes it pretty damn special." I sealed my lips on hers. In seconds, we'd thawed each other, and only warmth was between us.

Her kiss wasn't tentative. It was sure. An answer without words. And despite all the awful things that had happened lately, I'd never been happier.

Woof.

Woof. Woof.

Sadie barked impatiently, which only added to the rightness of the moment.

"It is pretty damn special," Pepper whispered.

She tucked her hand in the crook of my arm and we strolled to the rescue.

"Miss Adeline always says everything will work out fine," she said as I put my hand on the door handle. "I used to have my doubts, but now I believe she's right."

And those words were almost better than an *I love you* back.

Almost.

CHAPTER TWENTY-SEVEN

TEAGUE

"DAD WANTS TO SEE YOU."

Lincoln appeared in the mailroom. I checked my watch. It was nearly midnight.

"What the hell? He sent you to fetch me? At midnight?" I finished sorting the stack of envelopes in my hand.

He pressed his lips together, clearly unhappy about the situation. That made two of us.

I loosened my tie and moved toward my brother. We fell in step on the way to the elevator.

"Why do you do whatever he says?" I asked while we waited.

Lincoln stared straight ahead. "Because it's easier."

There were deep-set lines spidering out from the corners of his eyes. He looked like he hadn't slept much lately, though he hadn't ever needed much sleep anyway. My brother was generally stoic and hard to read, but even he had trouble disguising that he was worn out.

"I don't see how." And I would never fully understand being at our father's beck and call. I loathed every second of giving in to him.

"Did the attorneys think you have a case?"

I'd filled him in on the bare basics earlier in the day. And I wouldn't have gone to see a lawyer without talking to my brother about it. We hadn't had time to get into the details.

The elevator doors opened, and we stepped inside.

"They do." I leaned against the back wall. "I'm not sure why I'm pursuing it when I'm stuck here until Dad decides I'm done."

Lincoln flicked his eyes toward the camera in the corner in warning. The longer our father didn't know about my legal suit, the better, but he already knew I wasn't going anywhere until I was sure he'd leave Pepper alone.

We stopped on the lobby level, and Beau breezed in. She stumbled, startled, and put her hand over her heart. "What are you doing here?"

She stepped forward and the doors closed.

"I work the late shift, remember?"

She glared and straightened her wrinkled dress.

"Where have you been?" Lincoln lifted a brow, intimidating in a way only he could be.

"Nowhere." Her answer was quick and sharp. "Have you been promoted?"

I hesitated a moment. She was deflecting. I couldn't decide if I wanted to let her get away with it. "I've been summoned," I finally said.

Worry turned her lips down. "Lucky you."

"I thought you were headed home for the night." Lincoln wasn't so easy on her.

"You thought wrong. Where are we on the Park property? Has the seller responded to the offer yet?" More deflection.

I pulled her into a sibling embrace. She squeaked, caught off guard.

"I'm so glad you're back." The faint scent of cologne hit my nostrils.

She whacked me in the chest but didn't try to get away. "It's temporary."

"I'm getting in good with boss." I smirked. "He might listen if I tell him you need to stay."

She smacked me harder. "You wouldn't dare."

I laughed. Like our father would take into consideration anything I said. It was tempting to try so I could keep my sister around longer, but I wouldn't do that to her. If she was happy a million miles away, then I was happy. Sort of.

Ding.

The elevator doors opened on the top floor.

Lincoln pulled me aside as I forked off toward the office of doom. "Whatever he wants, don't argue. He'll just make your life even more of a living hell."

Was that possible?

Images of Pepper's distraught and brokenhearted face bombarded me. The rescue closed and the dogs headed for the pound. Yes, it could absolutely get worse. This, staying, was for the woman I love.

I nodded, though I wasn't sure I could stick to that plan.

"What's he want?" Beau's mouth flattened.

"Don't know."

She nibbled her lip. "Are you done for the night after this?"

"Don't know that either."

She rolled her eyes. "If you are, let's all ride home together. Unless you aren't going home."

I hadn't mentioned anything to Pepper, but it had almost become a given whenever I had a free minute, I went to her. Because I loved her.

I still couldn't believe I'd told her that, but I was glad I had. I never wanted her to doubt how I felt.

"You just got here."

Thank goodness Lincoln didn't notice the birds chirping and the hearts dancing above my head. I'd much rather the focus was on Beau than on me.

"If I'm not stuck here all night, we can ride home together," I said.

She sent me a silent look of gratitude. "Good luck."

"I need all the luck I can get." I started down the hall.

"Teague," Lincoln said when I'd only taken a step. "Don't let him get to you."

I released a long, steadying breath. "I'll try."

There was no secretary to chase me at this hour. The double doors were closed when I approached my father's office. I didn't bother to knock. He'd summoned me. He should expect me.

I stepped across the threshold but couldn't bring myself to walk any farther into the room. "You wanted to see me."

I hated all I did lately was give in to him. How he must love having me fall in line.

This is for Pepper.

The reminder kept me from saying something smart.

"Don't play games, son."

I balled my fist. He didn't deserve to use that term with me. If he thought I'd call him Dad to his face, he had another thing coming.

"I'm not the one speaking in riddles." I yanked on my tie, unknotting it completely.

He glowered, and I got some small satisfaction from annoying him.

"You have no chance of winning a lawsuit against the city of New York."

How did he know I'd met with Zegas and Whitley? I'd barely had a chance to tell Lincoln, who I confided in about everything, and I *hadn't* talked to Beau yet.

His scowl turned into a smirk. I'd let my thoughts translate to my expression apparently. Another point for him.

"Your place is with this company. You will not disgrace the Hollingsworth name with a frivolous case."

So this was about him and his precious name.

Too bad for him I didn't give a damn about it.

"I'm here working for you just like you wanted. The rest of my life is off-limits." I folded my arms.

"Not when it affects your family."

"Beau and Lincoln support me no matter what I do." I hoped to make it clear he was not part of my family.

"It would be a shame—"

"Save your threats." I was tired of them. I'd told Lincoln I'd try to keep my cool, but I was failing. Our father was under my skin and sending my simmering blood to the boiling point. "I've done everything you asked. We made a deal. I'm holding up my end. Are you going to be a man of your word?"

I already knew the answer. I'd known when I agreed to work for him. He kept moving the goalpost and would continue to because he'd never be satisfied.

Would I continue to allow him to?

I'd have to until I outsmarted him. As shameful as it was to admit, I hadn't yet.

"Don't test me. It won't end well for those mutts."

It took every bit of strength I had not to fly across the room and throttle him. A reaction. That was what he wanted. If I reacted, he had every excuse he needed to do whatever he wanted. Was anything stopping him now?

Hell, no.

As we stared at one another, I realized I'd made a drastic mistake.

I never ever should've given in to him.

He was the puppet master and held all the strings. When he tugged, I danced.

When the truth hit me square between the eyes, I wasn't sure who I hated more.

Myself. Or him.

CHAPTER TWENTY-EIGHT

PEPPER

"IT'S SUPPOSED to rain the day of the fundraiser."

Vivian tossed her phone on the table in disgust.

"I thought you had a backup plan." I glanced around the mostly empty room.

Paths of Purpose was a shelter for abused women and children. When I'd had nowhere to go, I would've given anything for a place like this.

It was clean and welcoming, like a home.

Millie sniffed around in search of crumbs from her position under the table. She'd already made herself at home.

I looked around again. I'd been leaving Miss Adeline alone at the rescue too much lately, but she'd insisted I come. A partnership between Paths of Purpose and Grey Paws was too important to continue to put off.

"So sorry to make you wait." A woman in a sleek pantsuit with her hair pulled back in a low bun rushed over.

Millie sat up and edged closer to my leg.

"We had some last-minute details to go over for the fundraiser anyway," Vivian said.

I hadn't come to terms with the event yet. Fortunately, I hadn't had much time to dwell on it.

"I'm Audrey Quinn." The woman took the chair across from us.

"This is Pepper." Vivian introduced me, and I appreciated it.

"Nice to meet you, Mrs. Quinn." That was what Vivian referred to her as, so I followed suit.

"Lovely to meet you too."

"This is Millie," I said, pointing under the table. She'd put her head in my lap. I stroked her head.

She was so good with Eric, I decided to bring her along as a test. As any dog might be, she was a little nervous being out of her normal circle of familiar places. Every minute she was here, she became more comfortable.

"Hello, Millie." Mrs. Quinn held out her hand. Millie sniffed, then licked, giving her a stamp of approval.

"I've spoken to a lady who runs a rescue upstate. She works with a prison in her area." My face heated. "I don't mean to insinuate your facility is like jail," I said quickly.

Mrs. Quinn offered me a kind smile. "I know you didn't. Those kinds of programs can give us a guideline as we form our own."

"Yes." Relief filled me. Thank goodness I hadn't insulted her. "Eventually her dogs stay with the people involved in the program. I don't know if that's something you'd be comfortable with here, but for me, we'd have to work toward it."

"Agreed. When we built the shelter, we didn't plan for the possibility of therapy dogs." She shook her head. "That feels like a major oversight looking back."

"We've never done anything like this," Vivian said. "And if the preliminary program works, then we can deal with reconfiguring."

"Until recently, we didn't allow pets." Mrs. Quinn took a sip of coffee. "After seeing what the dog did to bring new life into the shelter, we began to think of possibilities. This seems to be falling into place."

I appreciated her enthusiasm. Vivian's topped all of ours, and it was contagious.

"My biggest concern is logistics. There are only two of us at Grey Paws. Until the dogs and the ladies get used to each other, I wouldn't feel comfortable dropping off our dogs for hours or letting them spend the night."

"I wouldn't either," Mrs. Quinn said. "The beginning stages would be a time commitment for all of us, but our goal is to create the least amount of stress all around."

"Maybe it would be best for the residents to go to the rescue at first. Or maybe we split it. Half the time they go there and the other half the dogs come here. Since some of the ladies need to stay close to Paths." Vivian tapped the tabletop with her finger.

"That's not a bad idea." I warmed to it. That seemed more doable than hauling our dogs here all the time.

"We should start slow. One day a week perhaps. Let's ride with training wheels." The more Mrs. Quinn spoke the more comfortable I became.

"We can do a half day a week," I said. In my head, I pictured the dogs needing more of an adjustment period than the humans, though that might not have been fair. All of them had been through some sort of trauma. They already had a connection to build on. And not only that, we couldn't have a group of women just arrive on site and need to be entertained for a whole day. "I'm thinking that maybe just one or two women could come initially. And perhaps ask around to see which women would most like to go. From my experience, women who are frightened of dogs often cause the dogs around them to be just as nervous, and sometimes the anxious dog would act out."

"Aggressively?" Mrs. Quinn asked.

I smiled. "Not intentionally, and if we just bring out the calmer dogs into our front room, those who have been with us for a little longer and have happy human interactions, we should be fine."

"Oh good. That sounds manageable."

"And dogs do sleep a lot during the day too, so they may only have an hour of entertainment in them." I rolled my eyes, which made Mrs. Quinn and Vivian laugh.

"Our new van arrives late next week. A trip to the rescue would be the perfect maiden voyage." Mrs. Quinn was practical and thoughtful.

"Should they go to you or to us?" Vivian asked.

I hoped in a couple of weeks, all of our dogs would be back together again. "Let's plan on the rescue. Any day of the week works for us, but I'd recommend sometime after breakfast and before dinner. Mealtimes get kinda hectic."

There was a reason I hadn't let Sadie tag along today. That girl would've already investigated this whole building. I absolutely adored her stubborn self.

"We have the makings of a plan," Mrs. Quinn said. "Would you like a tour of our facility? Or do you need to get back?"

"I'd love to have a look."

"This is going to be perfect." Vivian clapped her hands, ever the optimist.

Mrs. Quinn stood and nodded. "I have a feeling you're right."

CHAPTER TWENTY-NINE

TEAGUE

"YO. Thought I might find you here."

The doorbell chimed as Burke walked into Grey Paws. I hadn't spent the night here, but as soon as I'd gotten up, I'd headed over.

"I had no idea you liked me so much you'd search the city for me." I slapped his hand and pulled him in for a bro hug.

"He's here for me," Miss Adeline called from the back.

"You know it, sweetheart," he hollered back.

A few dogs rushed over and swarmed his feet. He stooped to pet them as they jockeyed for position.

"What's up?" I motioned to the desk for him to sit on in case Miss Adeline came back to her chair.

The piece of furniture creaked with both of our weight on it. Under our full weights, it probably would have collapsed.

"Guess you need to lay off the donuts." He punched me in the arm.

"I'm not the only one."

I missed the constant ribbing of the guys.

His expression turned serious and he lowered his voice. "Ellen got the autopsy back."

I straightened. "Yeah? What did it say?"

My pulse thrummed faster. Burke had me believing in his murder theories.

"Heart attack. No foul play." He sounded disappointed.

I wasn't sure how the news made me feel. "Did Cassano have any underlying conditions we didn't know about?"

"Not sure."

"Any news on the other bodies?" Sometimes the tests could take time, which was frustrating when we wanted immediate answers.

"No." His shoulders slumped. "I asked Ellen to send over the report, but she hasn't yet. I just know there's a connection."

He'd circled back to Cassano. I got why he was so desperate to tangle all the fires and deaths together. That was easier to understand than the simple fact that bad things happened. We were used to seeing that every single day, though that didn't make it any easier to accept.

"We might never know." At least we had some answers when it came to Cassano. He was still dead, so I wasn't sure why it mattered.

"I talked to my friend at the lab. He's stalling, but I want to see the reports for myself."

"You ever think about moving over to the investigation unit?"

Burke was like a dog with a bone when it came to some cases. He wouldn't let it go until he had answers.

"Nah. They need my muscle on the front line." He flexed and pretended to polish his bicep.

"Get outta here." I shoved his hand away from his muscle.

"Jealous much?" He laughed his deep throaty laugh.

I shrugged. "A little."

Ding.

He fished in his jeans pocket and retrieved his phone. "That's my friend."

"The lab guy?" I peered over, trying to read the text.

"Girl," he corrected absently. "She wants me to meet up with her."

I furrowed my brow. "Like a date?"

He turned scarlet. "Hell, no. Like to talk about something she doesn't want to discuss over a text."

"Tell her to come by here." I wasn't ready for him to take off yet, though his shift probably started soon.

He pecked out a text and got an instant response. "She said she'll be here in twenty."

"Let's go grab some lunch from the deli." I jumped off the desk. "Miss Adeline, what do you want from the deli?"

"When are you going to start showing off these supposed cooking skills?" she yelled back.

I cupped my hands around my mouth. "I'll pick for you."

She appeared in the doorway. "No way. I want the sandwich with the caramelized onions. Tell them it's for me and they'll know."

"A little thing like you needs more than that," Burke said with a cheeky grin.

"I'll take a frosted cookie." She glanced behind her. "But don't tell Pepper or I'll get in trouble."

"Yo. Where is she?"

I hoped her long absence meant things were going well at Paths of Purpose. "She had a meeting."

Miss Adeline hadn't seemed surprised or annoyed when I'd showed up on their doorstep.

"Bring some chips too," Miss Adeline said. Muffy perked up like he understood what she said.

"Mind if we take Ash?" I'd never had her on my own, but in so many ways she felt like mine.

She tossed me a lead. "Better grab Pepper and the lab lady something too."

The snoop. That woman didn't miss anything that went on within these walls.

"Be back in a few." I leashed Ash, who patiently waited to move until I headed for the door.

"Will you watch for Willa in case she gets here before we're back?" Burke asked.

"Take your time." Miss Adeline smiled mischievously. "I need a minute to do some of my own investigation."

.   .   .

THE DELI WAS SLAMMED, and by the time we returned, Miss Adeline had already settled in, pumping Burke's friend for who knew what kind of info.

Pepper stuck her head out of the back as I set one of the food bags on the desk. "I hope you brought me something. I'm starved."

"Maybe." I crossed the room, no longer caring about lunch, and pulled her into my arms. "Hey."

She pressed up on her toes and chastely kissed me. "Hey."

"Teague and Pepper sitting in a tree. K-I-S-S-I-N-G," Burke sing-songed.

I turned to flip him off but thought better of it since we were in the presence of ladies.

"Grow up," I said.

He laughed. "Mind if I wash up?"

"Make yourself at home, honey." Miss Adeline pointed him toward the back.

We all followed to wash our hands, including the dogs . . . except Muffy who meandered innocently over to the bags of food.

"Don't even think about pulling a Sadie," Pepper scolded. He sat and pretended like he'd never thought about finding out what was for lunch. "Thank you."

She dragged a hard-sided dog crate from the back before washing her hands.

Miss Adeline sank back into her chair. "Willa, I'd suggest the dog crate or the desk. You definitely don't want to sit on the floor or you won't have any lunch."

"You might have some new best friends though," Pepper said.

"I'll take the desk. And thank you for the sandwich." Willa accepted the wrapped sandwich Burke offered her.

He settled in beside her. I took the end of the desk and Pepper sat on the dog crate. Sadie sat on one side and Muffy on her other.

"You know she's the one who drops food." Pepper flicked her chin toward Miss Adeline.

"Should we think about getting more chairs?" I asked before an argument escalated.

"It's probably not a bad idea," Miss Adeline said. "I'll call Beau. She'll know what to put in here."

"Would she mind shopping?" Pepper sipped her water.

I nearly choked on my sandwich. "Um, no. She'd be thrilled." And I hoped I didn't have to tag along again . . . although if she had one of those shopping plans she'd talked about maybe it wouldn't be so bad.

"Should we go somewhere private to talk?" Willa spoke quietly to Burke.

"Stay here so we don't have to strain to hear," Miss Adeline said.

Willa looked a little taken aback. The lab probably wasn't this lively.

"Nah. I'd tell them what you said anyway." Burke ripped off a massive bite with his teeth.

"Logan, I tell you these things in confidence," Willa snapped.

"And these are my people. I trust them."

That Burke trusted Pepper and Miss Adeline because I did meant a lot to me.

She pulled a stack of papers from her bag but didn't look at them. "I ran a tox screen on all the victims."

Something about her calling Cassano a victim struck me as odd. It was just a generic term, one that definitely fit the bodies in the barrels, but it felt wrong for him. He'd hate being referred to that way. Any of the guys at the firehouse would.

"Ellen said the autopsy proved heart attack." Burke chomped on his sandwich. A piece of lettuce fell from it.

Sadie raced and gobbled it up. She decided to stick around him since he seemed to be the most likely to drop something else.

"I'm sure it did," Willa said. "Tetrahydrozoline was in his system."

"Is that normal?" I twisted to look at her. "And what is that?"

She chewed on her lip. "Unless they gave eye drops to him in his water instead of his eyes, no, it's not. Though the amount is something that can be overlooked in an initial analysis."

"So it could be foul play." Burke perked up.

I put my sandwich down. "Is it possible that stuff was in another drug they gave him at the hospital?"

"Not likely." She thumbed through her papers. "On this case alone, I couldn't rule conclusively. There is an inordinate amount in his system, but he'd suffered other traumas due to the fire injuries. Mr. Cassano could've passed away as a result of the drug, but maybe not."

"You didn't have to tell me that in person." Burke hung his head.

"I'm not finished." Willa was no-nonsense. "Of the other five victims, I only had enough of their remains to test three of them."

"Five?" I asked. "I thought there were only three victims in the barrels?"

Burke looked behind Willa at me. "I had her look at the people from the fire you saved Cassano from."

Ash's fire.

I tore off a small piece of ham and discreetly fed it to her. Pepper noticed but said nothing.

"All of the victims had roughly the same amount of tetrahydrozoline in their systems. Given the timeline and proximity of the fires, the cases appear to be correlated. And this is why I wanted to tell you in person and not via text." Willa showed Burke the paper she'd pulled from the stack. "The cause of death is, without a doubt, homicide."

CHAPTER THIRTY

PEPPER

"WHY DIDN'T THEY KILL ASH?"

Burke and Willa had left hours ago, but we were all still shell-shocked. Willa's findings concluded that Ash's owners were deceased before the fire started.

Teague put an arm around my shoulders and pulled me close. "They probably thought she'd die in the fire."

I shuddered. It was impossible to think about Ash not being in our lives, yet we were so close to losing her. What if Teague had walked a few feet away from her? He might've never known she was there. And he'd gotten suspended for saving her life.

"Do you really think all these fires are connected?" It seemed impossible. I didn't know anything about serial arsonists or killers except oftentimes they had similar patterns for each crime. These seemed to be haphazard other than the heart attacks and the fires.

"It's possible." He rested his chin on top of my head. "We don't know who these people are other than Cassano."

"I can't make sense of why someone would've—murdered him." I stumbled over the word *murder*. "With eye drops. If it was the same person who hurt Ash's owners, it doesn't fit with the other victims."

"In an emergency situation, it's easy to miss clues, but I don't remember Cassano seeming familiar with the townhouse when we went to the fire." He scratched his temple.

"Maybe these people didn't know each other, but the person setting the fires knows all of them." I racked my brain trying to put together the few clues we had. Even though I had no true connection to any of this, I felt like I did because of Ash.

And the fire in the park felt personal.

"Could be . . ." He released me. "We have about three pieces of information. The locations. There were fires. And there were heart attacks."

"Why the long faces?" Beau appeared in the doorway in skinny jeans, an oversized sweatshirt, and a long gold necklace. Her version of casual was my dressed up.

"Why aren't you in the kitchen?" Lincoln stepped behind her.

She wheeled around. "Because I don't cook."

"I know that." He rolled his eyes. "I meant Teague."

"We just finished feeding the dogs," Teague said.

"Let's go upstairs and make sure Miss Adeline hasn't burned the place down." I snapped my mouth shut. Suddenly that phrase wasn't as funny as it had been before.

At the word *upstairs*, a pack of dogs raced up the stairs to the apartment.

"Thanks for having us over for dinner," Beau said. "Hope we're not throwing off your schedule."

"Not at all." I waved her off. "Glad you could make it." I leaned toward her conspiratorially. "I don't cook much either."

She high-fived me. "We can put our feet up and let the boys do all the work."

"I like that plan," Miss Adeline said as we piled into the house.

"Remember that grill you gave me for my birthday?" Teague slung an arm around his brother.

"I remember," he said cautiously.

"I got the box up here. Take off that jacket and tie and grab a screwdriver."

Lincoln scowled.

It was then I saw the big box by the balcony doors. When had he brought that over?

"I found all the tools you'll need." Miss Adeline picked up a box cutter off the kitchen table for emphasis.

Beau dropped into the oversized chair in the living room. "I thought we were eating sometime tonight." She kicked off her shoes and tucked her legs under her.

"If you helped, this would go faster," Teague said.

"No it wouldn't." Lincoln shrugged off his overcoat and suit jacket and laid them over the back of the couch.

They'd made themselves at home. There was a time I thought I'd feel territorial about that. This was my place with Miss Adeline.

Instead, I found I liked the extra boost of life they added. And somehow, it felt right. We hadn't opened up our lives to many over the years. We'd never had time. And yet, having these extra bodies here felt completely right. Like home.

"Open the box. I'm going to marinate the chicken." Teague rummaged through the cabinets.

"I'm not assembling a grill to eat chicken."

Lincoln once again surprised me. He seemed always in charge yet tended to go with the flow when it came to his siblings.

"I got steaks too," Teague said impatiently. Sadie barked. "What did I say?" He looked at me.

"An S-word," I whispered.

"I thought it was B-words that were off-limits." He pulled down a glass baking dish.

"All words are off-limits when it comes to that one." Miss Adeline patted Sadie's head.

"Don't you need that?" Beau motioned to the instruction manual Lincoln tossed aside.

He grunted and continued to pull parts out of the box.

"Who gives someone a grill they have to put together?" She winked at me.

Lincoln muttered unintelligibly under his breath.

"A jerk," Miss Adeline added. "But lucky us. We get to see men at work."

"Ugh." Beau wrinkled her nose. "Those are my brothers."

"You could call whoever messed up your dress to help us." Lincoln didn't look up when he delivered the jab.

"Do you already have a boyfriend here?" Miss Adeline asked hopefully. "You'll stay longer if you do."

Beau picked at the end of her sweatshirt. Teague turned around, interested in her answer.

"I definitely don't have a boyfriend."

"Give it a few days," Miss Adeline said. She wandered over to the other chair and sat.

I touched Teague's arm. "Anything I can do to help?"

"Make sure there's no bloodshed before dinner." He pulled down a few spices from the cabinet and some items from a grocery bag.

"I'll try my best."

I picked up the instruction manual and flipped through it.

Lincoln had all the parts separated. "She's right. Only a jerk would give someone an unassembled grill."

"But then you'd miss out on the fun of putting it together." I sat beside him.

"Move out of the way, handsome. She's a wiz when it comes to that stuff." Miss Adeline propped her feet on the sofa.

"Be ready to bring us drinks." I smoothed the instruction manual and studied it.

"I'm not as helpless as Beau makes me out to be," Lincoln said.

"When's the last time you put anything together?" she asked smartly.

"The bunk beds you had to have when you were eight."

She stuck out her tongue. "My point exactly."

"Hold this please." I stood one of the legs on end and screwed on a wheel.

"Are these all the tools you have?" Lincoln looked at the skinny collection consisting of two screwdrivers, a hammer, and pliers.

"We may have something else in the junk drawer." I attached another wheel to a leg.

"My toolbox is next door if we need it," Teague said over his shoulder.

"Should we tell dirty jokes? My mind just went in the gutter talking about toolboxes." Miss Adeline thumbed through a magazine.

"We are *not* telling dirty jokes." I shot her a warning look that she ignored.

"Do you have any tequila? A few shots and the really good jokes would fly." Beau picked up the fireman calendar from the end table.

"We are *not* doing tequila shots."

Apparently Lincoln and I were sticks in the mud.

"Can we have a beer or is that off-limits too?" Beau tossed the calendar away in disgust.

"Don't tell me you're anti-calendar too?" Miss Adeline looked appalled.

"Looks to me like they'll let anyone in that thing." Beau reached into her tote bag. "Let's redecorate downstairs."

She took her tablet and sat on the floor by Miss Adeline's chair.

"I said some chairs, wild woman." Miss Adeline closed the magazine.

"We'll see. I have a friend with an amazing shop. She'll have the perfect pieces." She held up the tablet.

"Don't forget whatever we get is going to be ruined." I scanned the instructions again. "Do you see this screw?"

Lincoln searched the plastic baggies and found the one I was looking for. "I'll do this side."

Teague towered over us. "Looks like I'm right on time. You're almost done."

"Hold this leg in place, please." I directed him where we needed him. I lined up a screw and tightened it. "It's your grill. Do you want to put the lid on?"

"I better so I don't get any grief that I let you assemble the whole thing."

I put the screwdriver in his hand. He tested the lid once he had it on.

"Where's the charcoal?" Lincoln stood and smoothed his pants.

"By the counter." Teague helped me to my feet. "Mind if I keep this on your balcony?"

I opened the French doors. "Not at all."

"If you aren't going to cook for us, then forget it," Miss Adeline said.

"Whenever you want."

Sirens wailed not too far away. Teague hustled outside and leaned over the rail.

"There's a fire two blocks away." He jogged through the apartment and out the front door.

Ash tried to follow, but I hurried and caught her before she slipped out. I went back to the balcony. Teague ran down the street toward the blaze.

My heart pounded. "He doesn't have any equipment." I looked at Beau helplessly as we watched him disappear.

CHAPTER THIRTY-ONE

TEAGUE

"ANYBODY INSIDE?"

A small crowd had gathered outside the building engulfed in flames.

"My grandmother. She saved me, but I lost her." A little girl tugged on my sleeve with tears in her eyes.

"Where did you last see her?" It was a long shot that the girl could remember, but I'd be better going in with a direction.

"On the stairs."

This was bad. I had no protective equipment, and I already felt the heat. The sirens grew louder, but every second counted.

I scoured for a way inside. The flames glowed from an upstairs window. Smoke billowed out the entry door, but that looked like the best way to go.

I jogged up the steps and tucked my face into the crook of my arm. The thick smoke stung my eyes. I forged ahead anyway.

The lights were still on in the hallway, though the light was distorted. Any minute the power could be cut.

I made out the stairwell in front of me and ducked low. It was awkward to try to protect my face and crawl. Time was too precious to turn back.

On one hand and my knees, I limped up the steps. The flames got hotter the farther up I went. I had to be close to the top and there was no one in sight.

The building was four stories and it was dangerous to press forward. The wood of the stairs scalded my hands and knees. Sweat poured down my forehead into my eyes. Smoke seeped into my lungs. I needed to move faster or I'd pass out.

I crept over the landing and ascended the next staircase.

My eyes burned as I struggled to stay low and see what was ahead.

Please don't be on the top floor.

I reached for the next step. My hand hit something. I felt around.

A leg.

Thank goodness.

Spurred by relief, I scooped up the form and held my breath. The smoke was thicker up higher when I stood.

Slowly, I descended.

It was impossible to see. I relied purely on instinct.

The person weighed heavy in my arms as I struggled to concentrate on getting us out of here. Flames licked the walls of the stairwell.

I stumbled.

Somehow I managed to keep my footing and hold on to who I hoped was the missing grandmother in my arms.

How many more steps?

I needed to breathe. A thick film coated my skin and nostrils. I ached for fresh air but ignored the strong urge to take a deep breath.

My feet hit solid floor.

Red lights flashed just beyond the fog. I rushed through the open door into the night and inhaled deeply.

A little woozy, I searched for a paramedic truck to take the person in my arms to.

"Hollingsworth." The sharp bark was familiar and unwelcome. "What the hell are you doing here?"

I strode past Captain. "You can't fire me again."

My lungs burned. My eyes felt like I'd stuck my face in a vat of chemicals.

"Yo!" Burke rushed over. "Let me take her."

I refused, almost to the back of the ambulance.

"Teague!" Pepper sprinted toward me.

I set the woman on a stretcher and turned to catch Pepper in my arms.

"I'm going to get you dirty." I held her tight.

"Are you crazy? You could've been killed."

Her words and clean air in my lungs cleared some of the fog in my head. I guided her toward the paramedics.

"Is she going to be okay?" I prayed I hadn't been too late.

"Did you find my grandma?" The little girl yanked on my pants leg.

I squatted and planted my fist on the ground to steady myself. "I'm not sure." I didn't know if I should show her the woman on the stretcher or not.

What if she hadn't made it? I didn't want the last thing this child saw of her grandma to be this.

Cough. Cough.

We both whipped our heads in the direction of the ambulance. Fingers wiggled on the hand that dangled off the stretcher.

The little girl tentatively approached. "Grandma?" She touched the hand coated in soot.

A head lolled to the side. "Sunshine?" The voice was scratchy.

The child threw her body against the stretcher, clinging to her grandmother.

"We need to get you some oxygen, ma'am." The paramedic gently placed an oxygen mask over the woman's face.

The girl's eyes widened. It was a scary sight, no matter what age a person was.

"We need to take you to the hospital for observation."

The woman vehemently shook her head. She moved the mask. "I don't have insurance."

I touched her foot. "Let them take you. Everything will be all right."

She began to argue, and I squeezed gently.

"Is there someone who can stay with you?" Pepper squatted so she was eye level with the girl. The child shook her head slowly.

"I can't leave her here," the grandmother said, distressed.

"She can come with us, ma'am." The paramedics loaded the woman into the back of the ambulance then helped the girl inside.

"I lost Edgar," the girl cried.

"Who is Edgar?" I asked, on edge. Had I left someone else behind? A boy?

"My stuffed dog." She sniffled.

"We'll try to find him. You go with your grandma." I nodded at the paramedics to close the door.

"You saved that woman, but you could've been killed." Pepper lit in before the ambulance was in gear.

Rivera nudged me in the arm. "Captain's hair is on fire because you're here. He's already called Chief. Maybe the commissioner."

I glanced toward Captain Koker, who was pacing with a phone pressed to his ear.

"What can they do?" I wiped the sweat from my brow.

"Have you lost your mind?" Lincoln stalked toward us with Beau on his heels.

"That building was engulfed. You're supposed to run away, not into it," she said.

"He's like a mule," Pepper said. "Forget trying to reason with him." She pressed closer to my side.

"You can't do things like that." My brother's voice was on edge. I half wondered if he was going to throttle me.

Burke emerged from the burning building and removed his mask. "Rivera. Grab that line."

Rivera jogged over to his abandoned post. He and Walsh aimed the water cannon at the flames. Scavino edged back the crowd that had pressed forward once more. People were always so curious. And some of them were scared.

There were tenants of this building watching their whole lives literally go up in flames.

As many times as I'd seen it, I still struggled to fully understand what it would be like to have nothing left but the clothes on my back. No one could sympathize unless they'd been through it.

Pepper knew.

Did this bring that all back for her?

When I looked in her direction, her focus was solely on me. Lines of worry were visible even in the darkness. When the strobe lights hit her face, they became more prominent. I'd caused that.

I didn't like it.

I took in the scene. Before Pepper, I'd had no one to worry over me. No one waiting at home to know if I was okay. Sure Lincoln and Beau would have been devastated if something happened to me, but I didn't picture their faces before I ran into a burning building.

I hadn't considered Pepper either.

The sirens had sounded, and I'd acted on instinct. Even though things were different now, that hadn't sunk in. I was still stuck in a past and a career that was no more. Zegas and Whitley might get my job back, but I couldn't take it. Not as long as my father remained my puppet master.

That woman could've died.

My brothers at the fire department had been minutes behind me. And that was all it would've taken to be the difference between life and death.

That little girl could've been left with no one. My family could've been left devastated.

How was I supposed to reconcile between those two scenarios?

I'd grown used to constantly putting others above myself. As much as it pained me to see the stress of the people I cared about, if I had it to do all over again, I'd go in for that woman without a second thought.

The flames lulled as the guys worked to put out the fire. Burke motioned for me.

"Be right back." I kissed Pepper's temple.

Burke looked over his shoulder and moved toward me. Captain was still occupied by his car with his back turned to us.

"I went in myself. No one else was inside," he spoke low with a hint of relief in his voice.

"That's good news." Every fire wasn't necessarily related to the others. Hell, we hadn't even proven all the others were connected.

As long as there was no one dead, that was a good thing. Buildings and belongings could be replaced. People couldn't.

"You did a good thing." He wiped his brow. "A stupid thing, but a good one."

I nodded. It was reckless and dumb. I couldn't deny my friend that. But when it was in my blood to serve and protect, what else could I have done? "Keep me updated."

"We miss your sorry ass." Walsh punched me in the arm.

"Better not say that too loud." I fist-bumped him. "I'm out."

"Take a shower," Burke said. "You look like a chimney sweep."

As I walked toward Pepper, Beau, and Lincoln, a dark car caught my eye. The lights flicked on as it eased away from the curb.

I'd seen that car at every fire lately except Ash's. Although, had it been there and I hadn't known to look for it? What was I missing? Maybe it wasn't so far-fetched they were all related after all. I needed to tell Burke about the car. I needed the answers and soon, because if it was here tonight, was somebody meant to die?

CHAPTER THIRTY-TWO

PEPPER

"FEEL LIKE TAKING A DRIVE?"

I'd suggested cereal again, but Teague had insisted on finishing the meal he'd started. While the grill heated, he took a shower.

The meal was amazing. He really could cook, and yet, everyone had been quiet after all the excitement, and I thought that had a lot to do with the fact that we'd seen Teague in action. His siblings knew he'd been a firefighter. I knew that too intellectually. But seeing the building on fire, watching Teague rush out with a body in his arms made his job very real. He'd been a hero. But he'd definitely taken an unwelcome risk. The silence—the tension—had been palpable, though Teague didn't seem to regret doing what he'd done. It made me wonder if we'd ever just have a relaxing night sometime in our future, as we'd certainly experienced our fair share of crazy since we'd met. And maybe, taking a drive was his way of finding something normal.

"Sure." I couldn't believe he'd be up for going anywhere but to bed. I was exhausted and I hadn't saved anyone's life today. "Let me tell Miss Adeline."

Lincoln and Beau had left a few minutes ago, and Miss Adeline had gone to get ready for bed. We still needed to walk the dogs.

I poked my head into her room and heard the shower. "Woman, we're going for a drive. Be back in a bit."

"Don't get caught fooling around in the truck. I've only got enough bail money for one of you."

I snorted. She was nuts.

"Are they okay up here?"

The dogs were out in a trail between Miss Adeline's room and the kitchen where we'd just finished washing dishes.

"They're fine."

He grabbed his keys, and we crept out, trying not to wake the dogs. The lock clicked as I quietly shut the door.

Woof.

I winced but tiptoed down the steps. Teague held the back door open for me. He made sure it was locked then secured me in the cab of his truck.

He cranked it up, and we rumbled down the alley.

It was late. The traffic was light. A lone person moved briskly along the sidewalk.

"Are we headed anywhere in particular?" I asked after a few blocks.

Teague drummed the steering wheel and stared straight ahead. When he didn't answer, I wondered if he'd heard me.

"I didn't mean to scare you earlier." He cruised through a yellow light absently.

"You did," I said quietly.

After he'd run off, we'd chased him. Watching him go in a building consumed in flames was heart-stopping. I felt like I hadn't taken a breath until he'd emerged. Seeing that woman in his arms had been a crash of emotions.

She might've died without him. What if *he'd* died?

I shuddered and tried to shove the fear out of my head.

"If someone needs help, I can't leave them behind." His voice was gruff.

There was something ingrained in him that went deeper than most. People ranged along the full spectrum when it came to helping others. He had an instinct to save people without thought.

Teague was selfless.

I admired and hated the quality at once. My hatred was pure self-ishness because I didn't like the way it made me feel to see him put himself in danger.

How many people were still living because of him?

He probably didn't know.

"I belong at that fire station," he said more to himself than to me.

It was obvious. I doubted he realized how hard of a time he was having letting it go. Who could blame him?

He'd had what he loved ripped away from him.

Now he was stuck because of me.

"Whether or not Zegas and Whitley get you reinstated, you need to quit your family company."

He jerked his head toward me. "I can't."

"If your father wasn't involved, would you want to work there?"

He focused back on the street and was quiet for a long time. "No."

"Then don't go back."

"I have to. He'll destroy the rescue—"

"We'll figure it out." I was terrified of what Mr. Hollingsworth would do and that hadn't subsided since Teague had struck a deal with him.

That niggling fear wouldn't go away. I couldn't live like that.

If we were all going to be miserable anyway, Teague shouldn't have to sacrifice so much.

"I'll handle him."

"He's working you to the bone with these crazy hours and demands. We have no more certainty about things than we did before you agreed to his terms. It's just a matter of time before he breaks the deal," I said in a rush.

"He knows I talked to the lawyers about getting my job back."

My eyes flared. "How?"

"Sometimes I'm pretty sure he's watching me. Maybe Zegas or Whitley is in his back pocket too," he said tightly. "He said I should think about our family name before I go forward."

"He's trying to take away what you love."

"I already lost it," he yelled. He eased to a stop at a red light and let out a long breath.

"Which is why you need to fight to get it back."

"My happiness is nothing compared to yours."

It was as if he'd hit me with a sledgehammer. That was love.

He'd said the words, and they still hadn't sunk in. But he proved with everything he did that I was the most important.

I didn't know what to do with that.

"I will have a love-hate relationship every time you go out on a call, but it's where you belong. Not stuck in a suit in a mailroom."

He gripped the wheel. "We need a plan. And if I'm not getting that job back, there's no reason to go through the hell he's going to rain down on us."

"You'll get your job back."

"How can you be so sure?"

I didn't have an answer for that. Except he was innocent. He'd been unjustly let go.

"I have faith."

He pulled over in front of a mansion but didn't turn off the engine. He kept looking straight ahead, almost as if he couldn't bear the sight of the house.

I reached for his hand. He didn't immediately yield to my touch. I tangled our fingers. His were calloused and rough from hard work.

"I keep seeing his car at the fires."

My grip went limp for a moment. "Whose car?" I asked carefully.

"*His.*"

"Do you think he's responsible?" Teague's father was a monster. I'd witnessed it time and again. That didn't mean he was capable of murder . . . did it?

"He'd never get his hands dirty," he said with disgust.

"Wouldn't it be stupid to go to the scene of the crimes if he does have anything to do with it?" My head spun.

The heart attacks.

The fires.

His father.

My stomach rolled.

Teague was a lifesaver.

His father was a destroyer.

"I normally talk to Lincoln before acting." His voice was stoic, detached.

"What are you going to do?" I squeezed his fingers.

"I thought if you were with me, it would stop me from wanting to confront him." He finally looked toward the house. "Stay here."

He pulled on the door handle.

I kept my grasp on him. "Teague?"

I mentally begged him not to get out of the truck. If his father was capable of . . . the worst kind of things, I didn't want Teague to provoke him. Standing up to a crazy person was useless.

"I won't be long," Teague said gruffly.

"Think this through."

"You sound like Lincoln."

"Then you should listen to us." I tugged on his hand.

He slid out of the truck. His movement was stiff and very un-Teague like. He turned and I lost my grip. His face was like stone.

"If I tell you to go, then go."

Fat chance. I yanked on my door handle and jumped out.

"You aren't doing this on your own."

That seemed to jolt him from his walled-off state. "I don't want you anywhere near him."

"Too bad." I marched up the walk.

He snagged me by the waist as I reached the gate. "No."

"You have no plan. You need backup." I fumbled for the latch on the gate.

High beams shined, nearly blinding me. I squinted. Teague shielded his eyes and stepped in front of me.

Once my eyes readjusted, a chill skittered up my spine. A sleek black car slowly rolled by. The windows were tinted so dark, I couldn't see inside, but I *felt* the eyes on us.

I held my breath as we waited for the vehicle to keep going.

It eased to a stop.

"Get. In. The. Truck." Teague nudged me.

I remained rooted in place as nerves got the better of me.

The back door of the car opened. A polished shoe gave way to a tailored suit.

Teague shifted me so that I was behind him. His urge to protect was ever present. I peered around and saw the worst.

CHAPTER THIRTY-THREE

TEAGUE

"YOU'RE SUPPOSED to be at work."

That was the car. I had zero doubt now.

Why was he at all the fire scenes?

Was he following me?

Or observing his work?

I tightened my jaw. What was I thinking, bringing Pepper here? My goal had been to make him forget her, not draw attention in her direction.

"Why were you at the fire?"

I hadn't meant to mention that yet. My temper got the best of me. What was the big deal? He already knew I'd seen him. The car always made a point of leaving after I'd discovered it.

"In case you've forgotten, you're employed by me." He stalked toward me. "*Not* a firefighter."

"One doesn't have to be a first responder to do the decent thing." Ugh. What little I'd been around him, he'd already rubbed off on me. I was speaking like him.

"Only a fool would've rushed into the blaze for a useless old woman. She'll probably die anyway."

I stiffened. Was he a prophet or would he make certain she died?

"She has a child she's responsible for," I said through my teeth.

"To what do I owe the pleasure of this visit?"

I tilted my head. He'd changed the subject like a champ.

My throat closed. I had no idea how to answer. Why was I here?

"I've already met your *girlfriend*." He spoke the word with disgust, like it was insignificant. Like Pepper meant nothing. "I don't need to see her again. You'll come to your senses soon about that too."

"By senses do you mean your way?" Pepper asked as she stepped out from behind me.

I resisted blocking her again. She didn't need me to protect her.

I wanted to. Especially from him.

"She's smarter than I gave credit for." He spoke as if she hardly existed.

"Answer the question. Why. Were. You. At. The. Fire?"

He smirked. "I was in the neighborhood."

Jackass.

"I don't believe you."

"Son, a good businessman keeps eyes on his assets." His gaze narrowed on me.

"And what about good fathers? What do they do?" Pepper's sharp tongue had come out to play.

I was so damn proud of her for saying the things I hardly had the courage to say.

He spared her a glance. "You wouldn't know."

She squared her shoulders. "You're right. I wouldn't. But you should."

"Most of my children are a reflection of me."

What a lie. None of us were like him. None. Of. Us.

If he believed little digs could affect me, he was wrong. Knowing he was disappointed in me was a compliment.

"Not that I've seen."

"Little girl, you must be aware that your world exists because I allow it."

Pepper and I paused. Was it really that simple? And if that were true now, her association with me had destroyed her independence. I wasn't sure I could live with that.

But I couldn't leave her alone.

"You aren't God." There was no reason to bother telling him not to insult Pepper. That would only make it worse.

His answering smile was sinister. "In this city I am."

A ring of truth was in his words.

"You didn't know me before a few weeks ago." Pepper had found her voice, and she sounded irritated.

"So small-minded."

I stepped closer. We were eye to eye. "*Don't* speak to her that way."

"Haven't you learned not to get attached? Your mother should've taught you that lesson."

A wave of rage crashed on top of me. "Why do you bring her up in almost every conversation we have?"

He flinched, and I swore under the glow of the streetlamp there was pain in his eyes. "She's the only way you'll listen to me."

"You aren't worthy to speak of her," I said through my teeth. *What does this man want? Why? Why does he do this?*

"This is not the way to get what you want." He remained ever cool and calm. The trace of pain I thought I saw a moment before had disappeared.

"As long as I'm anywhere near you, I don't have anything I want."

He canted his head. "That's not a very kind thing to say in front of your girlfriend. I was certain this was about her, although I'm happy to hear she isn't what you want."

Damn it. That wasn't what I meant, and he knew it. He was a master at taking advantage and twisting words.

"Are you going to say whatever it is you came here to get off your chest?" He continued as if bored.

I clamped my mouth shut. A million thoughts cluttered my head. What had I come here to say? Was it to let him know I'd seen him at the fire? Had I hoped for a confession?

No.

I'd acted on impulse in a haze of anger. With no plan, I had a sneaking suspicion I'd played right into his hands. He'd make me pay for this visit, though I didn't know how.

"Nothing else?" His tone was triumphant. "While I so enjoy our time together, I have things to do."

"What's more important than your children?" Pepper asked quietly. "You've wasted so much time you can't ever get back."

His hard gaze met mine. "I never went anywhere."

I did. Because of him and his rule with an iron-clad fist.

He didn't get to pretend like he was the wounded one.

Lincoln was. Beau was. I was.

"It didn't have to be like this." I clenched my fist. Pepper was right. We'd lost so much time and there was nothing to be done to repair the damage. He wasn't going to change and neither was I.

The reality I'd lived in for most of my life punched me in the face again.

I hadn't just lost my mother that awful day.

I'd lost my father too.

"You chose this path," he said hoarsely.

Always blaming me. He never had any responsibility for the position we were in.

"And now I'm choosing another." I glanced apologetically at Pepper. I prayed she meant what she said. That we could figure out a way to survive.

In the few days I'd worked for my father, he'd already sucked so much life out of me. If I kept on, there'd be nothing left. And that was exactly what he wanted.

His nostrils flared as if he could read my mind. "If you break your end of our deal, you'll force me to break mine."

"You would anyway." I couldn't stand the constant pushing of the finish line, especially when I was the only one doing the giving.

"Go to work."

Was his face red?

"Your days of controlling my life are done." I put an arm around Pepper's shoulder. "You'll leave her alone. I'm getting my job back. And you'll forget you ever had a second son."

For the first time since I'd caved in to him, some of the pressure on my chest released.

"You will always be my boy."

He spun and marched back to the car. Just before he shut the door, I caught a glimpse of someone else inside.

Captain Koker.

CHAPTER THIRTY-FOUR

PEPPER

I COULDN'T SLEEP.

Every noise set me on edge. How would Teague's father bury the rescue? I flip-flopped between fire and another horrible inspector.

I should get the dogs and Miss Adeline. Go somewhere and hide.

Hours after the confrontation, I'd had time for some of his father's mysterious words to sink in.

He knew I'd had no dad in my life. I'd been so tense, that hadn't hit me. As I lay wide awake, I couldn't stop wondering how.

And why?

I was a nobody in Samuel Hollingsworth's world. I preferred it that way. Yet he seemed to know things about me that even I didn't.

I felt invaded.

Like he was here without physically being around. He had this looming presence over everything. I had a feeling that was exactly how he liked it.

He was lording over our lives.

I was proud of Teague, but he'd pulled the pin on a grenade.

When I'd left Cope and lost everything, I'd lived with a constant fear. Selling my car had been terrifying. Then what little money I'd gotten vanished faster than I'd anticipated. My stomach had been in a constant knot of worry.

At some point after I'd settled in at the dog track, that fear disappeared. Or maybe I'd grown used to carrying it around.

It had been a long time since I'd been that scared. The unknown was worse than seeing disaster coming.

Now, everything was unknown again.

And that fear was back with a vengeance.

Back then, I didn't know how I'd ever get out of the deep hole I was in. I'd given up on ever having a place of my own. I hadn't dared to dream of where I'd landed with Miss Adeline. I lived moment to moment.

Survive.

That had been my only goal.

Now, I had so much more to lose. I had people and dogs I loved.

Before, I'd only had my pride.

I'd learned that wasn't so important.

Grey Paws wasn't a building. We could relocate anywhere and we'd still be us. But I didn't want to give up what we'd built.

I'd grown to love this city. It had given me a second chance. A place to grow and become the person I wanted to be.

In reality, it was Miss Adeline who had done that.

This was her home. I wouldn't let someone take it away. Not without a fight.

"We winged it." Teague's gruff voice was in my ear. "That's why I always got in trouble at the station. I couldn't stick to a plan."

He slung his arm over my stomach.

"Because most of the time no plan in the world can prepare us for real life." I snuggled farther under the covers.

"I was reckless tonight."

"You did what you should have done all along." While there was a weight of fear from the uncertainty pressing down on me, I was relieved Teague was no longer bound by the strings of his father.

"He's going to retaliate. And it won't be against just me."

"I'm scared." I didn't feel any better admitting that out loud. I felt weak.

"Me too."

I flipped on my side to face him. "You are?"

"I don't know what he's going to do. And I won't be able to stop it." He rolled over so we were nose to nose.

Sadie was on the pillows above us. Muffy and Ash were at the foot of the bed.

If it weren't for the dark cloud looming over our heads, things would be pretty perfect.

"I hate you ever went to work for him."

He absently rubbed circles on my back. "I should've sucked it up and kept going. I should've been stronger for you."

"No," I said sharply. "He put you in an impossible position. I appreciate that you stood up for us."

Teague very easily could've said screw it and left us to fend for ourselves. And we could make it without him. But it was getting harder and harder to picture life without him around.

"I've never quit before."

I touched his arm. "You aren't. You're doing what's right."

"What's right is protecting you."

My heart clenched. Miss Adeline was the only other person who'd ever put me first. It still caught me off guard that he did.

"Not if you're miserable."

He stilled his hand. "Have you slept at all?"

"No."

"I'm sorry."

Sadie raised her head. In the moonlight, her *be quiet* look was cutting. I patted her side, and she settled.

"Does he follow you all the time?" I lowered my voice so as not to disturb the queen.

"I-I'm beginning to think so." He sounded rattled.

I didn't blame him. His father seemed to take control freak to the extreme.

"How does he know so much about me?"

Teague stared apologetically. He started his soothing rhythm on my back again. "If it were anyone else but him, I'd think he was bluffing. Just making lucky guesses. But he's been doing his homework."

"Why?" That was the question that had played over and over in my mind. It was why I couldn't rest.

In Samuel Hollingsworth's world, I was no one. Insignificant. Except I took some of his son's time.

"Do you think he has someone set for you to be with?" I asked before Teague could answer my first question.

"Like an arranged marriage?" He laughed bitterly when I nodded. "Knowing him, I wouldn't be surprised. He's never mentioned it though."

"He seems to want to control every part of your life."

"He's always been that way." He touched his forehead to mine. "I don't know if he's harder on me than Lincoln and Beau because I don't conform, or if that's just my perception."

"He's awful." I sank my teeth into my lower lip. "This is going to sound crazy, but I think he genuinely believes he's doing right by you. That he's a good father."

He shrank into the pillow. "I'm the problem."

"That's not what I meant," I said quickly.

"In his eyes," he amended.

That was exactly how it seemed. Which was hard to wrap my mind around.

"What if he was responsible for those fires?" I'd posed the question before, and it was no less difficult this time. That was a heavy accusation. Serious. But everything pointed to his father.

"If he did, and I lead the department in his direction, it could be dangerous for whoever is investigating," he said flatly.

"You think he'd kill them too?" I asked incredulously. "If he's involved," I amended.

"He seems to have no regard for life." His voice was pained. I tried to imagine if one of my parents had done this. How I'd feel. I couldn't. It was too upsetting to think about. And yet, this was what this incredible, thoughtless man next to me knew. A man he believed was actually capable of heinous crimes.

"Who's next?" I dug my nails into his strong arm.

"I don't know." He pulled me closer. "I need to tell Burke, but I don't want to put a target on his back. Besides"—he hesitated—"I saw the captain in my father's car tonight."

I gasped. "The one who fired you?"

"The one and only."

My grip on him tightened. "Your father got you fired. To force you to do what he wanted."

Teague recoiled as if I'd slapped him. His mouth opened and closed several times. Once the initial shock subsided, realization dawned on his face. "And I played right into his hands."

The self-loathing in his tone was heartbreaking.

"Don't do that." I couldn't stand to see him hurting.

"What if I could've kept those people from being killed? What if he did it to get my attention?" Anger seeped from every pore in his body.

I swallowed hard.

Bzzz. Bzzz. Bzzz.

Sadie let out an annoyed sigh as Teague's phone lit up on the nightstand. He reached behind him blindly and checked the caller ID.

"Yo."

Based on his answer, I guessed it was Burke. Teague's brows knit and he put it on speaker.

"Sorry to call so early." Definitely Burke.

"I was up," Teague said gruffly.

"Willa was able to identify one of the bodies in the barrels." He didn't sound as happy about that as I thought.

"That's good news."

Maybe this was a break in the case. Hopefully it would unravel all our conspiracy theories that were beginning to seem not-so-far-fetched.

"I can't make a connection," Burke said in frustration. "Does the name Sally Mims ring a bell?"

My heart stopped.

"No," Teague said as if trying to think.

"I'll keep digging."

"Thanks for letting me know." Teague ended the call and tossed the phone between us. "Pepper? Are you trying to sever my arm?"

My fingers were curled around his bicep in a death grip.

Blood poured in my ears like thunder. My whole body shook.

"Pepper?" Teague sat up.

"Sally Mims is my aunt."

CHAPTER THIRTY-FIVE

TEAGUE

HER AUNT?

Like I was in a fog, her words slowly sunk into my brain. As they replayed in my mind, the more it rejected them. One of those people couldn't be Pepper's aunt.

"She died in a fire, right?" Realization hit me like bricks falling on my head. "That letter didn't say where . . ."

Pepper trembled violently in my arms. "The house burned down."

"That doesn't mean they were in it."

She covered her mouth with her hand. A long, thick silence descended upon us as reality set in.

We likely didn't need DNA to identify the people in the other two barrels.

I understood what it was like to lose a parent. But I couldn't begin to guess what she was going through since she'd been lied to all her life.

In a way they were strangers, yet she had a connection to them anyway.

Maybe that was why I still allowed my father in my life on a limited basis. Because we were family. By blood. DNA only.

That seemed like a stupid reason.

What if I'd never known him? What if I never had the chance to know him?

Would I be the same person?

It was impossible to view life without him in it. He had this looming presence that never went away.

Had Pepper's parents been tucked away in a back corner of her mind? Could she miss someone she'd only seen pictures of?

I stroked her back in jerky movements. What was I supposed to say? *I'm sorry your aunt was murdered and my father probably had something to do with it.*

This was a nightmare. Just when I thought it couldn't get worse . . . it did.

"I don't understand." Pepper reached for Sadie. "How did they end up here? Is this because of me?"

I thought carefully before I spoke. "We don't know the motivation."

"My circle is so small," she said as if she hadn't heard me.

In the shock of the news, maybe she hadn't come to the same conclusion I had about my father. The more we learned, the more likely it seemed he was involved. Which meant these deaths weren't just a message to her.

They were a message to me.

I was responsible for the loss of Pepper's family.

And then it hit me. That was why he'd had them put in the park. Because it was a special place to her.

He'd set it all on fire.

So I'd fall in line.

These deaths would hurt her, but he'd started with her outer orbit. He was getting closer and closer, which meant his next move would be more painful.

"I—" I cleared my throat. "I think this confirms my father's involvement." My voice was ragged. He was a monster. I didn't want to believe he was capable of this.

"How?" She rubbed Sadie behind her ears.

"He has the motivation. To get me to do what he wants, he targeted you." I hadn't pieced together how Cassano or Ash's owners fit, but they did. My gut screamed that it was all connected to me.

I'd caused death and destruction even if I hadn't struck the match.

"We didn't know who they were until now. How does that get you to do what he wants?" She sounded far away, like she couldn't think clearly.

"He knew we'd figure it out."

Her hand fell back to her side. Sadie pawed at her head, and Pepper petted her again.

"I'm numb." She begged me with her eyes to make sense of the situation. "I should feel more."

"These past few weeks have been a shock to take in."

She snorted bitterly. "When does it stop?" Pain twisted her features. "I'm not sure I wanted to meet my parents, but now I'll never have the chance. I'm angry at all of them, but I didn't want them to die."

She buried her face in the pillow. What she thought was numbness was really an onslaught of too many feelings. I, too, was wading through a myriad of emotions.

Pain for how hurt Pepper was.

Anger that innocent people were dying. That Pepper had been dragged into something that ultimately was aimed at me.

Determination to stop this madness.

Fear that I wouldn't be able to.

"They didn't care about me. None of them." The torture in her voice clawed at me.

I held her close and kissed the top of her head. I didn't have the words I desperately needed to comfort her. But what could I say? What could anyone say? Until my mother's death, I'd had a good home life. And then even though I lost my mom, I still wasn't alone. Lincoln had been my rock. Beau had been my joy, often a light in a dark time. Pepper had been so alone. For so long. It wasn't right.

It wasn't fair.

She sniffled. I hooked my finger under her chin. In the moonlight, the shimmer of tears reflected back at me.

It was wrong, but I wanted to stuff my father into a barrel and set him on fire. He'd hurt her. He had to pay.

But an eye for an eye wouldn't fix this. It wouldn't take away all the damage he'd done.

There was nothing to change what had happened that would make it any better.

Not even his death.

"I underestimated him," I said against her hair. They weren't the right words to stop her tears. They weren't the right words for the moment. But she allowed me to be who I was. The me very few people knew.

"You defied him."

I wiped away the tears that leaked down her cheeks. "I have to tell Burke. It's the only way I know to stop him."

"Pointing the finger in his direction won't do anything. Especially if he's not the one actually murdering people and setting them on fire," she cried.

Muffy lifted his head and put it on her leg.

"It might slow him down." She was right. Obviously my father didn't care if we knew what he'd done. He seemed to be taunting us.

Pepper shot out of bed and went to the window. "Someone could be out there right now."

I moved behind her and wrapped my arms around her middle. "I don't want you to worry about this."

She spun and tilted her head back. "How can I not?"

I cupped her cheek. "I don't know. I just—I want you to be able to live your life like normal."

"There is no normal life anymore," she said. "Normal now is wondering where the next fire will be and who's going to die."

I cradled her against me. That was the brutal truth. I couldn't dispute it, and I wouldn't disrespect her by trying.

I could still hope.

Bzzz. Bzzz. Bzzz.

Someone's phone vibrated near the bed, but neither of us moved.

The first rays of light highlighted the edge of the sky. It was too early for more bad news.

The noise stopped and immediately started again.

"I don't want to answer," I confessed.

"Just get it over with."

Lincoln's name flashed across my screen when I picked up my phone off the nightstand. The fear that seemed to be my constant companion flared.

"Hey."

"Dad's in the hospital." He spoke neutrally like he'd been awake for hours too. "Massive heart attack."

CHAPTER THIRTY-SIX

PEPPER

THE PHONE FELL from Teague's hand onto the bed.

"What's wrong?"

Ash edged closer and nosed his thigh.

He stared at me helplessly.

"My father had a massive heart attack."

I grabbed the bedpost to steady myself when I swayed. We'd been so sure he was responsible for all the evil swirling around us.

He was horrible.

Despicable.

That didn't make him guilty. It didn't make him worthy of suffering a heart attack.

It would be easy to think that. All the evidence pointed to him. But even with what we knew, there was so much we didn't. So many puzzle pieces that were simply confusing. Had we been wrong about his dad earlier though?

"I'll go with you to the hospital." I searched in the dim light for my overalls.

He didn't move. "Why would I go?"

I stepped in front of him and grabbed his arms. "Because if you don't and something happens, you have to live with it."

"He doesn't deserve any of us being there."

I couldn't argue with that. "Don't be like him."

Something about my words seemed to shake Teague. He swiped his jeans off the floor and tossed them onto the bed. He shoved off his sweats, and I resumed my search for my own clothes. Now wasn't the time to be distracted by his perfect body.

The dogs were on alert. Both of us petted them in between changing clothes.

Sadie barked.

Teague kissed the top of her head. "It's not time yet."

I loved that he understood and accepted her. All of us.

Tap. Tap. Tap.

The doorknob turned. "Everybody decent?"

"Yes," I called.

"I was hoping the answer was no." Miss Adeline poked her head in and frowned. "Why are you up before the sun?"

"Teague's father had a heart attack."

She straightened. "Go. I'll see about these hooligans."

I kissed her cheek. "Thank you."

"Aren't you proud of me? I didn't say something inappropriate," she whispered.

"Guess an old dog can learn new tricks." I hugged her.

She patted Teague's arm. "Let me know if you need anything."

He kissed her cheek too, and she squeezed him back.

Ash trotted to the front door right behind us. Before he opened it, he squatted and stoked her head. "We'll be back soon."

BEAU RUSHED toward us when we found them at the hospital. She flung herself into Teague. He caught her and wrapped her in a bear hug.

"I hate hospitals," she muttered against him.

I agreed. Strangely enough, this was the first time I'd ever been in one. Fortunately, neither I nor anyone I was related to had ever had cause to go. I'd never had grandparents who might've needed a trip.

And Miss Adeline was up in age, but she was healthy. All her doctor appointments were in an off-site office.

I'd seen them on TV, but this one was brighter white. Everything was white except for the specks in the vinyl floor and the few pictures dotted along the walls. It smelled weird even though it was spotlessly clean.

Beau released Teague, hugged me, and led us over to Lincoln, who was on the phone speaking in a hushed tone. He wore the same expression as always. Stoic stone.

He flicked his chin in acknowledgement.

"Winston found him lying on the stairs. He's critical," Beau said quietly.

She sounded almost detached. Not unfeeling, but not with the emotion one might normally have if their father was in serious condition. Although, I had no experience with what that was supposed to feel like either.

If it were Miss Adeline, I'd be a mess.

They were all . . . neutral.

"You didn't have to come," Lincoln said as soon as he ended his call.

"I'm here for you two." Teague's response was stiff.

I linked my fingers in his in silent support. This had to be hard on him. Coupled with the events of the past few weeks, it was just icing on the worst cake ever.

He hadn't said a word on the drive over. I'd let him have the space to sort out whatever was going through his mind.

His father had kidnapped me. He might have had something to do with murdering my—they weren't really my family—aunt and parents.

Yet I couldn't find it in me to wish Samuel Hollingsworth ill will.

Strangely, I felt detached from all that had happened. Fear had dominated me for weeks. Not for the things that had occurred but for the things to come.

I hadn't let myself think about the horrors as if I had some sort of mental shield in place protecting me.

Was that how it was for these three?

"Why are we here?" Beau muttered, catching me by surprise. It was hard to figure out exactly how she and Lincoln felt about their father.

I never sensed they liked him particularly, but it wasn't the same as Teague, who clearly despised him.

Their father was like a wound they'd all learned to live with.

"Because even when he's on death's doorstep, he's still pulling the strings." Teague looked down at the floor.

What was this power their dad held over them?

If my parents had come back into my life, would I have let them, even after they'd abandoned me? I'd never know. They were strangers to me. I'd lived too much of my life without parents that I simply couldn't wish for them to be anything to me. There were only times that I'd wondered if I'd taken after either of them. Facial aspects, personality traits. Goals.

There seemed to be some deep-seated need in human nature to have a relationship with our parents, no matter what they did. Maybe it was because we wanted them to be something they weren't.

Teague had every reason to shut his father out completely. He probably should.

But I respected that there was something in him that held out hope even if it was in vain. Because if we gave up on the worst people, that meant they couldn't change. That the world couldn't be a better place.

And if it couldn't, why were we all here?

"Winston?" Teague motioned over to a man who appeared around the corner.

He appeared uncertain as he approached, like he wasn't sure he belonged.

Beau tucked her arm in his and leaned her head on his shoulder. "Thanks for being here."

Lincoln shook his hand but said nothing.

"I almost waited to call emergency," he said gruffly, as if he couldn't bear to admit that. "He's a crotchety old bastard, but he's taken care of me for over forty years. Did you know he paid my mother's medical expenses?"

Teague tightened his grip on my hand. How terrible it must have been to hear that his father had treated people who weren't his flesh and blood better than he had his own children. How was he supposed to reconcile the man we'd confronted hours ago who was horrible with the same one who paid someone else's bills?

"You did the right thing."

Everyone jerked their heads toward Teague. He was a good and decent man. It took a strong person not to spit in the face of their enemy.

"I think I need to sit," the man said.

I held Teague back as they made their way to a nearby seating area.

"Are you okay?" It was a stupid question, but I needed to know.

"Not really." A troubled look flitted across his face. "If my father had a heart attack, does that mean he's not behind the killings?"

CHAPTER THIRTY-SEVEN

TEAGUE

I COULDN'T LEAVE the hospital.

It was crazy. Stupid.

I'd been here for three days and still hadn't figured out why.

I hated my father.

Was I sticking around to make sure he died?

No.

Even after the way he'd treated me and the people I loved, I didn't want him to die.

What kind of twisted person did that make me? His strings on me were wound tighter than I knew.

He didn't deserve to have anyone in a hospital lobby for him. He deserved to be alone.

Yet I stayed.

I rested my elbows on my knees and dropped my head.

My mother would've wanted me here. And that was part of my motivation. I wanted to please someone who was never coming back in case she was watching from somewhere above.

As much as I loved my mother, pleasing her wasn't enough.

I couldn't describe the reason. It was just rooted within. I didn't want my father to be a bad guy.

He was. I wouldn't deny it. But the memories of when I was young were strong. Then he wasn't awful to us. Distant at times. *Not* the unfeeling monster he'd become.

I was the one who ultimately cut off communication . . . because he'd forced me to. We'd reached an impasse that we hadn't gotten past in almost twenty years. All the bitterness and hurt hadn't evaporated because he was in critical condition.

I certainly wasn't rethinking my actions. There were some things I could've done differently, but I wasn't the one in the wrong.

I'd wished more times than I could count that things would've been better between us.

Watching the monitor giving him life didn't erase the things he'd done. It didn't earn him my automatic forgiveness.

It had earned him some of my time.

The nurses hadn't allowed me to sit in his room until a few hours ago. Automatically, I'd followed them when I wasn't sure I wanted to be there. They assumed I was a dutiful, heartbroken son, desperate for his father to make a recovery.

I wasn't sure how I felt.

Was there something in my nature with a need to save people? *Is that why I'm here?*

"Want some coffee, honey?" A nurse spoke low as she entered with a Styrofoam cup in her hands.

"Thanks."

She offered me a couple packs of sugar and powdered creamer. I accepted all of it, though I wasn't sure I could handle anything to eat or drink right now.

She fussed about my father, checking the machines and his vitals. I watched without really seeing, exhausted from the bits of rest I caught every once in a while.

I should leave. Lincoln would be here soon. Besides, my father had no idea I was by his side anyway.

"Talk to him," the nurse said. "It helps more than you can imagine." She pulled the door closed behind her when she left.

Talk to him.

There was nothing to say. It wouldn't make me feel better to get any of this off my chest because it wouldn't change things. Not just because he wasn't listening. Even if he were, he was who he was.

"Am I dead?"

I jerked my head up at the sound of his scratchy voice. It was as if he hadn't spoken in a year.

"No."

"If you're here, I have to be or hell has frozen over." His dark eyes didn't have the sharp glint they usually held.

"I was thinking the same thing." I rubbed my hands up and down my thighs.

"You look like shit."

I gripped my knees. "That's really what you want to say to me after almost dying?"

His color was off. He'd been out for several days, yet he didn't look frail. Just maybe not as mighty as usual.

"Where are Lincoln and Beau?"

I dropped my chin to my chest. Had I not been giving myself a stern talking to about how he'd never change? In my naïve mind, I must've believed he'd wake up a different man.

"Not here." I could've told him they'd be here soon but was in no mood to bring him any comfort.

"Because they care about the company. You should take a lesson from them."

I struggled to rein in the anger threatening to explode. He didn't deserve to see how he upset me. I had to stop allowing him to do it. At this point, it was on me.

"The company doesn't care if you die or not."

"You don't either."

I wanted to look away from the challenge in his gaze. Always with the mind games.

"Then why am I here?" I spat.

"You know you've been wrong—"

I shot to my feet. "I've been wrong?" I lost control of the volume of my voice. "*I've* been wrong?" I repeated incredulously. "I chose an honorable career and you couldn't support me. You're my father. You don't have to like all my decisions, but you're supposed to be there."

"I've shaped you so you can survive."

"You're furious I don't do what you say," I growled, temporarily forgetting we were in a hospital.

"You have a role to play in this family." He coughed, the first sign of weakness since he'd woken up. Only my father would come out of critical condition swinging.

"You aren't my family." It hurt to say those words even though they were true.

"I've tried everything. I thought you might listen to your brother and sister, but there's no reasoning with you."

I grabbed the bed rail. "You kidnapped the woman I love. You've threatened her. Threatened me." I leaned over him. "There is no reasoning with *you*."

"Sir! Back away from Mr. Hollingsworth." The kind nurse who'd just brought me coffee was now tugging on my sleeve.

I stalked to the window and plowed a hand through my hair.

"Leave us." My father's stern words weren't to be argued with.

Her shoes squeaked on the linoleum floor as she scurried away. He'd either have her fired for having no backbone or be pleased she did what he said.

I kept my back to the man who had been a looming shadow over everything I did. Sometimes I felt it and sometimes I didn't, yet it was always there.

"I needed your attention."

I spun. "Really? There are other ways to go about it. Like pretending to listen to me. Pretending to care."

He had a way of looking indifferent without being so. What was simmering beneath his surface, I'd never figure out. I could've dealt with the coldness if there'd been some grain of caring in his actions.

"You've put me in a terrible position."

I flicked my gaze to the monitors and shook my head. Always blaming me.

I drew in a breath and studied his form in the hospital bed. This was the most vulnerable I'd ever seen him, and he was still terrifying.

I yanked on my hair again. "I don't know why I stayed." It was another mistake. At least when he was out, there were no more ugly words and deeds. Now that he was back in the land of the living, the terror would start all over.

"You know I'm right." He coughed again, and the beeps on his monitor sped up a fraction.

"Are you okay?" He didn't deserve the question, but I didn't want to witness another parent die. An image of my mother as she was shot invaded my brain. The pain was acute and fierce.

"You're like her." The statement was low. He looked surprised he'd spoken it aloud.

"That's the nicest thing you've said to me in thirty years."

The beeping slowed again to a steady pace. I sank in a nearby chair, drained from the constant state of turmoil. I couldn't live like this. I needed peace. I needed Pepper.

"What do you remember about that day?"

Thank goodness I hadn't touched that coffee. It would've soured in my stomach.

I slid down in the chair. "Everything."

"Except who murdered her." There was frustration and relief in his voice.

"Why did you give up on finding out who did it?" This was the most persistent person I knew. I'd never understood why he'd let it go. Why the case was still unsolved.

"I didn't."

I straightened and leaned forward. "You know who did it?"

A few days ago, I would've thought it was possible he had killed her the way bodies were piling up. Now, I had no clue. Had he gotten vigilante justice? If he had, we'd just found something we could agree on.

"Nothing changes. She's still . . ."

I waited. I knew the end of that sentence. What was odd was he couldn't finish it.

"Gone."

He closed his eyes. For a minute, I thought he was back out. "Don't try to remember who murdered her, son."

"I thought that was what you wanted?" He'd been so angry when I couldn't. The details of the face were so fuzzy. It was as if I couldn't focus on them, and I'd been trying all my life.

"Come back to the company. I'll overlook your disobedience."

I white-knuckled the arm rests. He always cut off a conversation he didn't like with an insult.

"I'm not a child."

"And I won't let you suffer the same fate as she did."

He had no control over that unless he'd pulled the trigger himself.

"It makes no difference to me, but if you love that girl as you say you do, you will get away from her as far and as fast as you can. I assure you, living without her, knowing she's still breathing, is a far better fate than the alternative."

I stood again. "Are you threatening her again?"

He was out of control. Near death in a hospital bed, he was still dictating our lives like he was God. He did not sound like a man who had just been unconscious for three days after a heart attack. His words still contained such venom.

"I'm telling you how to protect her." Bullshit. He didn't care about Pepper. Why did he want me away from her? Why her?

My brain worked overtime. All the pieces of a puzzle I couldn't make fit scrambled in my head. I'd seen and talked to Pepper periodically over the past few days. She'd been supportive of my choice to stay at the hospital, easily setting aside her own feelings about my father.

How had he known I wouldn't leave his side?

I pulled out my phone and dialed Pepper's number. All the worst-case scenarios blared louder with every unanswered ring.

"What did you do?" I asked as the call went to voicemail.

"Nothing," he replied coolly.

Had my father faked a heart attack as a means of distraction? To get my attention and get me away from Pepper?

"What. Did. You. Do?" The pounding in my chest felt dangerous. Pepper.

I had to get to her. I had to see that she was okay.

Bzzz. Bzzz. Bzzz.

I nearly collapsed in the chair when her name flashed across the screen.

"Are you okay?" I asked gruffly as I moved to the windows, away from my father's listening ears.

"I'm fine. Why?"

I could picture her tilted head, a loose strand of hair from her ponytail hanging in her face.

"Just be careful."

I didn't want to scare her, but I didn't want her to be careless either.

"What happened?" What sounded like a metal bowl being set on the counter came through the line.

"He's awake."

"Oh."

Bark. Bark. Bark.

I checked the time. It was six. Dinnertime.

"Can I call you back? You know she won't be quiet until she's fed," Pepper said over the noise.

"Yeah."

All of my energy rushed out in relief. She was safe. I was overreacting because I'd been so on edge for weeks. My nerve endings were like live wires.

The phone buzzed again. *Did Pepper forget to tell me something?* I answered without looking at the screen.

"Hey."

"This was the easiest case I ever took." Zegas's cocky tone blasted in my ear.

"What are you talking about?" I'd forgotten about the lawsuit. With everything else happening, it had been the least relevant.

"I sent a letter to Chief Jones. He thought you'd resigned."

I leaned against the windowsill. "Resigned?" The word was foreign on my tongue.

"Yep. Resigned. When I explained how you'd been wrongfully relieved of duty, he reinstated you," Zegas finished triumphantly. "How am I supposed to charge Elliott triple time when he handed me a slam dunk like this?"

I snorted. The man was half insane but damn good at what he did. "So I'm back on?"

"He said to tell my client to get his ass to the station tomorrow night for duty." Now, that sounded exactly like Chief Jones. *Cranky bastard.*

My father watched me carefully as I tried to control my reaction.

"I can't believe it."

"Your record has been wiped clean. He said after taking a look, most of it was bogus anyway." Zegas just kept delivering good news.

I wasn't exactly looking forward to seeing Captain, but I could avoid him. The guys were going to be shocked. Hell, I was.

"Thank you," I said, still stunned.

"I hate to admit it, but if you'd talked to the man yourself, you probably wouldn't have needed me." He actually did sound like it pained him to say that.

"I appreciate the work you and Whitley put in."

"Whitley didn't do a damn thing. I do all the work. He's around for the glory."

What an odd pair they were. "You both got another win."

Slowly, it sank in that I had my job back. I couldn't wait to tell Pepper.

We hung up, and I fired off a text to her with the good news.

"Don't go back." My father had listened to every word. "Go flip burgers. Bum around. Just don't go back to the fire department."

I paused. That expression was still neutral, but his tone held a rare edge. He hadn't demanded I work at Hollingsworth Properties. He was right. Hell had frozen over.

"It's what I love." I didn't owe him any explanation, yet I'd been honest anyway.

"Loving something gets you killed."

CHAPTER THIRTY-EIGHT

PEPPER

"CONGRATULATIONS."

I wandered down the street with Sadie, who was oblivious to the cold. She moseyed, which was fine because it gave me a minute to talk to Teague. I dropped my phone in my pocket.

"Thanks." His voice warmed me through my earbuds.

I'd missed him while he'd been staying at the hospital, but I understood.

"You don't sound excited." I thought he'd be happy. Thrilled, really. Maybe the news hadn't hit him yet.

"I'm just exhausted." He sounded drained.

He couldn't have been getting much sleep, not to mention all the stress he'd been under.

"What can I do?"

Sadie sniffed a light pole like hamburger, steak, and pepperoni were scattered around it. No amount of coaxing could get her to move on.

"You're doing it."

"I'm walking the most stubborn dog who ever lived. I'm not sure how that's helping you."

Sadie looked back at me over her shoulder, and I swore that girl smiled at me. Because she knew I was talking about her.

"That's normal. So it helps."

I longed for some semblance of boring and routine. Miss Adeline might like action, but I'd had enough of it lately.

"How's your dad?"

He snorted. "How can a man have a massive heart attack, be out for days, and wake up as vicious as ever? He might be released tomorrow."

"You're kidding." He'd been critical. So bad that the doctors had been preparing Teague, Lincoln, and Beau that he wouldn't make it.

"Nope."

Something muffled through a loudspeaker was in the background.

"Are you staying until he gets out?"

He sighed. "I don't know."

I couldn't stand the struggle he was going through. He was being ripped in two for reasons I wasn't sure he understood. His father was awful, but Teague was wonderful. He wouldn't leave him alone. It wasn't in his nature.

"Have you talked to him?"

"If you could call it that. I just wish we could have a normal conversation. He could start by apologizing to you."

I pictured him in those white halls with his phone pressed to his ear, pacing. "I don't need an apology." If he left us alone that was all the *I'm sorry* I wanted.

"He owes you that."

"It wouldn't change anything." What was done was done. It was the future that mattered.

"He wouldn't do it anyway."

It sounded so trite to compartmentalize my kidnapping like that, but what other choice did I have? Even more traumatic things had happened since, and if I focused too hard on the anger I saw in Hollingsworth's eyes, I'd probably fall apart. So, no, I refused to give that man another ounce of my pain or fear. His apology would be words I'd ignore.

I finally coaxed Sadie to keep moving. Who was I kidding? She'd grown bored with the lamp post and decided we'd press on.

"I've been thinking a lot about family over the past few days," I said, hugging the front of the buildings to let a woman pass.

"Yeah?"

"I'm trying to feel what I'm supposed to about my aunt and my parents." I flipped my hoodie onto my head. "But that doesn't make sense."

"What *do* you feel?"

I thought for a minute. "I'm sad they died horrific deaths." I hoped they'd had heart attacks before the fire, though I wasn't sure. Technically, I didn't know if the other bodies were my parents, but it was an . . . assumption. It was surreal enough that it had been my aunt in one of the barrels, so all I could assume was that if one was her then the others could have held my parents. As bizarre as that could be.

"I'm angry they lied to me. They robbed me of the choice of knowing my parents. I'd have liked to have decided if I wanted them in my life."

It felt good to say that out loud. And once again, Teague listened without interrupting or adding his opinion. That encouraged me to go on.

"I might have shared blood with them, but they weren't my family." Pain stabbed at my heart. The truth hurt, but I'd rather face it than be in denial. "I'm thankful my aunt gave me a place to grow up. And I'm pretty much over how we left things. People make mistakes. They say things they don't always mean. My life here is a thousand times better than it ever was there."

I wished I'd had the kind of relationship with my aunt that I did with Miss Adeline. But Miss Adeline was one in a million. The bond we shared was unique and rare. I wouldn't have given it up to go back to Cope.

"I don't understand why they were killed. Was it the choices they made, or does it have something to do with me?" I tugged on the leash so Sadie would stop at an intersection.

"It could be both," Teague said.

Maybe it was.

"I guess what I've figured out is that it's okay for people not to be in your life, even if they're blood." I looked both ways before we crossed the street. "I don't mean that we shouldn't make an effort, but —" I tried to find a way to phrase my thoughts. "I like the family I've chosen. And that's okay."

I winced. "Does that sound heartless?"

"No." The background noise had faded.

"I shouldn't feel guilty or pay the consequences for their choices." That might have been some of the anger talking, but I had enough weight on my shoulders. I'd never know why they did what they did. Worrying myself over things without answers was wasteful.

"You're the calm in the chaos." He spoke quietly. Reverently.

I realized I liked to be needed. Maybe it was because before the rescue, no one ever had.

"I haven't figured out why I can't leave the hospital."

Now it was my turn to listen. And I would as long as he wanted me to.

"Part of it is because I have to know I did all I could. Which is crazy. He doesn't deserve one more second of my time."

While I hadn't been paying attention, Sadie had led us to the park. The scene had a new meaning since finding out my aunt had been in the barrels. It was still a charred black hole.

"I need to just cut the ties once and for all." He sounded hurt as he spoke. "It's the best thing for me. But I can't let go of the bitterness."

We allowed family to be part of our lives because we were supposed to, no matter what they did. Wherever that unwritten rule came from . . . it needed to go back.

"I can't hate him either. I should for everything he's done, but I can't."

I wanted to be with him. To be his shoulder to lean on.

Instead, we were in our own separate hells. If we could push past this time, we'd be in a better place.

"If you hated him, it would consume you. Not him."

Sadie stared at the remains of the park. What was going through her mind? She seemed to be taking it in, trying to figure out why what used to be there was no more.

"He has been consuming me anyway. I didn't realize it, but he's always there. I want peace, whatever that looks like."

I tugged on the leash, ready to go home. "You'll find it."

"I hope so."

"DID YOU GO BY GARRISON'S?"

Miss Adeline sat behind the desk surrounded by dogs.

"With Sadie? No way." I loosened her leash, and she wandered toward the others, barging her way into the space she wanted.

I flopped onto the desk and let my legs swing. I needed a minute before the next walk to warm up.

"I don't know why he wants the dogs to taste test his treats for the fundraiser. They'll eat anything." She shrugged and moved some papers around.

A corner of the fireman calendar appeared.

I touched it. "You're still looking at that thing?"

"And you're still offended by it."

"Not as much as I was." I tilted my head. "I'm not enthused about Teague posing again."

"When's he coming back?"

I fiddled with the edge of the worn wood. "Not sure. His dad's awake. They may let him out tomorrow."

"I thought he was critical." Her brow furrowed.

"Guess he came out of it." It was a miracle or maybe a testament to the man's stubbornness. He wouldn't leave this earth before gaining an iron-fisted rule over his family.

"I want whatever they gave him in case I ever have a heart attack." She tossed a ball and Millie retrieved it.

I cut my gaze to her, which she ignored. "What did you offer him? To get him off our backs?"

She threw the ball a few more times and avoided looking at me. "Something of value to him."

That wasn't evasive at all. "What?" I couldn't think of anything she had that Samuel Hollingsworth would want.

"This building."

I stilled my legs. This was the home she'd made with her husband. They'd restored it, had life and love here. We had a home here. She loved this place.

"Why would you do that?"

She folded her hands on her lap. "I panicked. I thought I could reason with the devil and we'd be done with him." She pressed her lips together. "It doesn't work like that."

"You love it here."

"I do. But I love you and the dogs more. I have the memories from this place and no one can take those away from me." Millie dropped the ball on top of her hands. "We have an alternate plan now too. Maybe we could talk the Elliotts into one of those fancy apartments in their building."

"*Woman.*" I reached for her hand. She placed her old one in mine. "You shouldn't have done that."

"My reasoning was right, but it was a mistake. I only handed him more leverage. I'm too old not to know better."

It was rare to hear her admit she was wrong. Although I wasn't sure she was.

"What made you think he'd want this building?" Other than real estate was his business.

She squirmed, and I narrowed my eyes. "Did you know"—she cleared her throat—"that he owns every building on this block? And most of the next one too?"

I gaped. "You didn't think you should bring that up before now?"

"It's public record, if you're willing to do a little investigation into the shell companies." She released my hand and threw the ball again.

"But if he owns all the property . . . that means—" I blinked at her.

"Teague's father is his landlord."

CHAPTER THIRTY-NINE

TEAGUE

"YO, Rivera. Am I losing my eyesight? Or am I seeing Hollingsworth putting his crap in a locker?"

I'd barely set foot back in the station and the ribbing had already begun. It was good to be home.

"No glasses needed, boys. I'm back." I slung my bag into the metal bin and locked it.

"Does Captain know?" Burke slapped my shoulder.

Rivera and Walsh did bro handshakes with me.

"If not, he's about to find out."

My father had been released from the hospital a few hours ago. I hadn't determined if that was doctor's orders or my father simply doing as he pleased like always. After I'd showered and stopped by the rescue to say hi, I'd headed for the chief's office.

Our chat had been brief. I wasn't in the business of complaining or trying to make others look bad even when they'd wronged me. Maybe that was why I was uncomfortable with hiring a lawyer in the first place.

If Captain had treated one of these guys the way he had me, I'd have fought for them with everything I had. They only knew what little they'd seen. I tried to keep the rest hidden. No need to worry them when they had their own families to be concerned about.

Bottom line was, from this point forward, any reprimands or punishment had to be run by the chief first. Basically Captain Koker couldn't touch me anymore.

He could still make my life hell, but I wouldn't be fired again without good cause.

Or unless Chief retired and Captain Koker replaced him. What I still didn't know was who controlled whom? Was it my dad or Koker who was leading the other by a tight leash? Both of them made my blood boil.

"You sure you don't need to go through training again?" Walsh pinched my side. "Looking a little soft."

I glanced down. I hadn't put on weight. I'd hardly eaten in the past few days.

They burst out laughing at my frown.

"Pretty boy's worried about his appearance," Rivera said.

"He's got a woman now. He better be." Burke made a catcall noise.

I punched him in the arm. "I haven't missed you assholes at all."

"Hollingsworth." Everyone straightened immediately at Captain Koker's shrill bark. "You aren't to be on the premises."

"You might want to talk to the chief about that." I decided smirking might not be a good idea. The man was still my boss.

His nostrils flared, and he turned on his heel.

"That went well," Walsh said as soon as the door slammed behind Captain.

"At least he's not out here anymore." Rivera high-fived him.

"I'm going to see what you knuckleheads did to my kitchen." I headed in the direction of my favorite place in the firehouse.

"While you're in there, whip us up something to eat. All we've had is crap since you've been gone." Burke smacked Rivera in the back of the head. "No offense."

"None taken." Rivera slapped him in return.

"We better do safety checks on the truck." Walsh motioned toward the garage.

Rivera groaned. "Great. You coming, Burke?"

"Be there in a minute." He flicked his chin and followed me to the kitchen.

"Have you heard anything about that lady from the fire the other night? The grandmother?" I asked. In all the chaos, she'd temporarily slipped my mind.

I tensed as I waited for the answer.

"Yeah. She was released the next day."

I almost sagged in relief.

"Were you afraid a heart attack got her?" Burke certainly didn't mince words.

"I've got good reason," I said.

He lowered his voice as I rummaged around in the cabinets. These guys had everything in the wrong place. "Willa was able to get DNA from another one of the barrel bodies."

I paused. "Got an ID?"

"I can't remember the first name, but it was the same last name as the other woman." I looked away and winced. I didn't know either of Pepper's parents' first names, but with the same last name, it was almost impossible it wasn't them.

"Find out if you can." I set a pot on the stove. She already knew, but I hated having to confirm the worst to Pepper.

"Any suspects?" I opened the fridge and gagged. "Don't any of you know how to throw stuff away?"

I slammed the door and shuddered.

"Yo. We've been a little shorthanded around here," Burke said in defense.

One man down was hard enough. Two? It would've been a struggle.

"Dinner is going to be late."

I held my breath and threw anything that looked suspect in the trash. So basically I emptied the entire fridge.

"We ain't been by the store either."

That figured.

"Help me haul this garbage to the dumpster, and I'll run to the market."

He grabbed a trash bag in each hand. I followed him with a couple more.

"Shit, that stinks," he said, as he heaved one into the dumpster behind the station. He caught my arm when we'd finished. "There's a set of the same prints at every scene."

"Is there a match?" And why was I just now hearing about this? Oh. I'd been holed up in a hospital for days.

He glanced around nervously. "Yeah. But I ain't saying who yet."

"Who is it?" If we knew—if we knew, I could confirm or rule out my father's involvement.

He rapped me on the head with his knuckles. "Did you not hear what I said? I'm not saying anything until I'm sure."

"You've got the prints," I said incredulously.

"Shh." He put his finger up to his lips and glared. "Keep your voice down, big mouth."

"What's the big deal if the guys hear?"

He grunted. "Just don't say anything."

"I wish you hadn't told me." I stalked back inside. "That's like saying there's a chocolate cake right there and I can't have any." I pointed to an invisible spot on the fire truck's gleaming bumper.

"You're good at pouting."

"Burke, you gonna help sometime today?" Walsh yelled.

"If you jackasses would throw out your trash occasionally, I already would be," he called back. "Between the three of you, it's a wonder I have any hair left."

"What did I do? You're the one keeping secrets," I said in a low voice.

He looked around again. "Fine, but if you breathe one word of this to anybody—"

"I wouldn't."

He knew that. Otherwise, he wouldn't have kept me up-to-date with what Willa found.

"It's—"

BRRRRRIIIIINNNNGGGG!!!!

CHAPTER FORTY

TEAGUE

I WAS RUSTY.

The alarm bell rang, and it took me a second to sprint into action. I threw on my gear and loaded in the truck, though I felt like I was behind everyone else. Things I used to do without thought weren't so quick to come.

And I'd only been gone a couple weeks.

I put on my headphones.

The siren wailed as we raced from the station.

Oxygen. Helmet. Ax.

Hopefully this was just a small fire to ease back into the routine.

"Three alarm. Residential and commercial." So much for a small fire. "West Seventeenth."

I seized at the announcement over the comms.

Grey Paws was on West Seventeenth.

I tapped Burke. "What's the exact address?" I yelled as we bumped down the street.

He looked at his phone and didn't respond.

"What's the address?" I repeated, panic setting in.

He shook his head.

This beast couldn't get there fast enough. I fought the urge to throw Walsh from behind the wheel and take over. We were only a few blocks away and every bit of my training was forgotten.

All I could do was pray Pepper and Miss Adeline had taken the dogs somewhere on an adventure.

I checked my watch.

Almost six o'clock.

Suppertime.

Please be okay, Pepper.

That one thought was on repeat as images of smoke, dogs, and chaos invaded my brain.

"One minute out."

A thousand lifetimes went by in that one minute. Flames blazed from the second story like an orange inferno in the night sky.

I'd seen this scenario more times than I could count. But this time was different.

The truck hadn't quite rolled to a stop when I jumped out. *I'm coming, Pepper.*

Burke was on my heels. "You aren't going in there."

"The hell I'm not." No one could stop me.

"Hollingsworth. You're outside." Captain Koker's voice was somewhere far away in my ears.

I could get fired for this. Legitimately. And I didn't care.

Burke grabbed my arm but wasn't strong enough to do more than slow me. "It's not safe for you to go in. You're too close personally."

"What would you do?" I challenged.

He let go and fell in step beside me.

"Make sure the dogs are out. They should be in the back. I'm going upstairs." I yanked on the front door handle. Locked.

I smashed through the glass with my ax and ducked through the opening. Thick smoke dulled my vision. I scanned for any furry bodies on the floor as I made my way to the staircase.

At least I knew this place with my eyes closed.

"Go." I pointed Burke toward the sound of barking dogs, torn between helping him and pressing on.

If any of them were in the apartment, the window of time was closing quickly.

At the top of the stairs, flames shot from the entrance. This was a situation we weren't supposed to run toward.

I'd die to save Pepper. And if something happened to her, I might as well be dead.

I took the steps two at a time.

Sweat leaked into my eyes as the heat intensified. I fought through the sting with only one mission.

Find Pepper.

As I neared the top, I had to walk through fire. These floors were wood. Any minute they'd burn and collapse.

"Hollingsworth, check in."

I barely heard Burke over the roar in my ears.

"Upstairs. Get the ladder ready."

"Six dogs clear. How many?" A hint of relief wound its way through me.

Please be out for a walk.

"Should be eight and two people."

My visibility was zero by the time I crossed what I thought was the threshold into the apartment. The living room, or at least in the direction of what I thought was the living room was a solid wall of fire. It danced toward the kitchen. If I didn't hurry, there would be no exit but to jump.

I'd never been scared on a rescue call. Not when the floor collapsed with Cassano or the dozens of other near misses in my career.

For the first time ever, I was terrified.

"Pepper!" I yelled as loud as I could, but my voice was swallowed over the roar of the blaze.

If they were in the living room . . . no, I wouldn't think about that.

I pressed farther into the apartment. The glow of my flashlight reflected off the cloud of smoke.

You're running out of time, Teague.

"Pepper!" I prayed with all my strength to anyone who was listening that they were safe. "Pepper!"

I heard barking and it was close. But where? Which dog? Because if I found one—

Something hit my legs.

I knelt and a familiar set of wild eyes met mine.

Oh shit.

Sadie.

CHAPTER FORTY-ONE

PEPPER

"STAY WITH ME."

I covered Miss Adeline's nose and mouth with a sweatshirt to block the smoke. We'd been stuck in my bedroom for far too long. I didn't know what to do.

The door was impossible to open. I'd raised the window, but I knew nothing about fires. There was something about oxygen. I couldn't remember if it was good or bad for the flames.

Smoke billowed under the door.

My eyes burned.

My nose burned.

My lungs burned.

Ash and Muffy paced from one corner of my small room to the other. Nervous. Panicked.

And Miss Adeline could barely keep her head up.

The sirens had been a welcome sound, but the fire seemed to have escalated at too rapid a clip to stop it.

I was out of options. The door was jammed shut. How? Sadie . . . where was she? Was she hurt? The other dogs . . . locked downstairs. Oh God.

We'd been about to feed them and then suddenly everything had gone up in flames. But how?

They'll find the dogs first.

Unless the fire started downstairs.

Oh no.

I couldn't think like that.

Cough. Cough.

The sweatshirt wasn't much better than nothing over Miss Adeline's face.

Ash sat next to her but close enough that she was almost on top of her. We were next to the open window. The smoke pouring out into the night made it almost impossible to get fresh air.

I stuck my head out. "Up here!"

My voice sounded little more than a whisper, clogged from the smoke. There were two firemen fighting the blaze with a hose. I tried again and waved my arms.

Why don't they see me?

A fireman burst out from the building with two dogs in his arms. He carried them over to a vehicle I couldn't see.

Thank goodness. At least they're safe.

I screamed again, but it was as if I had a muzzle on. The sound was muffled and weak. I beat the windowsill in frustration and yanked my hand back.

Hot.

I glanced behind me. The sweatshirt had fallen from Miss Adeline's hands. Muffy lay beside her and wheezed.

My head felt like it was about to split in two.

I rushed over and knelt next to her. "Miss Adeline?" I held the sweatshirt up again, but it felt like a monumental task.

Everything was heavy.

"Miss Adeline?"

No response.

I closed my eyes in hopes of stopping the burn. *Just for a second.*

I shook the woman I adored. It was almost out of body, like everything was in slow motion.

"Miss—"

CHAPTER FORTY-TWO

TEAGUE

How the dog was still breathing in this smoke was beyond me. I hustled to keep up. She ran past where Miss Adeline's room had to be. Just a little farther.

Woof. Woof.

In front of Pepper's door was a large piece of furniture. What was that doing there?

I placed my hands around the edges and shoved with all my strength. It screeched across the floor.

Crackle. Crash.

I spun. Through the smoke, it was impossible to see, but I was almost certain part of the living room had collapsed. I'd heard the sound enough times to make an educated guess.

You're running out of time.

I smashed the ax into Pepper's bedroom door over and over. Sadie leapt through the splintered wood and pawed at me from the other side.

I followed her toward the window where a clump of people and dogs lay.

"Pepper!"

No response.

Crackle. Crash.

I looked behind me. Flames engulfed where I'd stood only moments before.

I crouched. Miss Adeline, Pepper, Muffy, and Ash were all huddled together, none of them moving. *No. Please God, no.*

Sadie jumped and nuzzled and pawed them like she had on an oxygen mask.

Thank you, girl.

She'd led me to them. I glanced behind me again and my gut sank. The fire was dangerously close. I wasn't even sure I could retrace the same path I'd taken. If I could, there was a problem I'd never faced before.

I could only save one of them.

CHAPTER FORTY-THREE

TEAGUE

"SECOND STORY WINDOW. Need the ladder now."

I couldn't properly communicate. Everything in my mind had faded except figuring out how to get my family out of this building alive.

I waved my arm out the open window.

"Yo. I see you." Burke pointed up.

Walsh navigated the ladder toward me.

Woof. Woof.

He's not moving fast enough for me either.

In a normal situation, we removed the person in the worst shape first. In this one, it felt like having to pick a favorite.

Burke crawled up the ladder. I scooped Miss Adeline and carefully transferred her to his arms.

Crackle. Crash.

Fire consumed the doorway where I'd stood only a few moments ago. There was no other way out.

Hurry up, Burke.

The rug just inside Pepper's bedroom ignited and fire raced in the direction of her bathroom.

"I've got you." I lifted her lifeless body from the floor.

Her chest moved up and down, but it was slow and unsteady.

"Hang on for me."

I wanted to take her down the ladder myself. I never wanted to let her go. But I placed her in Burke's outstretched arms.

"Three dogs left."

Crackle. Crash.

It was as if the fire was chasing us. Where the door to Pepper's room had been seconds ago was now open space. Like tentacles, the flames licked closer and closer.

I couldn't keep an eye on the fire and if Burke had gotten Pepper to safety.

"Come down, Hollingsworth," Burke shouted through the comms. "The building is about to go.

"Not without the dogs."

Sadie dropped to the floor beside the window.

No. No. No.

I will not let you die.

Burke hustled up the ladder. I handed him Muffy. Rivera was down the ladder just behind him. Burke handed the dog off, then held out his arms for another.

I swallowed hard as I gave him Ash's very still body. Hadn't she been through enough already?

Please be okay.

I assessed how I could get on the ladder with Sadie in my arms. It would be tricky. She was too big to carry under one arm, and I needed a free hand to climb.

Crackle. Crackle.

Heat was at my back, Burke was only half way down with Ash.

Crackle. Crackle.

The only part of Pepper's bedroom that wasn't ablaze was this small corner by the window. That wouldn't be the case for much longer.

I picked up Sadie, who was frighteningly silent.

Burke scrambled up the ladder.

I all but threw the dog at him as the heat intensified.

Crackle. Crash.

"Hollingsworth!"

I leapt as the floor beneath me gave way and hooked the end of the ladder with one hand.

It jolted.

Burke stumbled.

I watched in slow motion as he lost his footing.

Somehow he managed to hold on to Sadie and the ladder. He righted himself.

A string of curses came through the comms.

I dangled from the end of the ladder. If I didn't have on this gear, it would've been easy to pull myself into the right position. I couldn't shed any of it and still hang on.

Pepper. I have to get to Pepper.

I mentally counted down from three and threw my leg onto the side of the ladder. The oxygen tank was like a weight on my back pulling me in the wrong direction. Toward the ground.

Stay calm.

My heart raced. Worry about the people and animals I loved consumed me. *I should've told her.* Even if she couldn't hear me, *I love you* should've been the first thing I'd said to Pepper. To all of them.

The memories we'd built in the short time we'd known each other went up in flames behind me.

We'll build new ones.

If you don't get off this ladder you won't.

"Yo. You need some help?"

Through our face shields, Burke's cocky smirk gleamed.

"I don't think I'm cut out to be a gymnast."

The ladder retracted. *What is he doing?*

"Walsh said if you're gonna fall, he wants it to be a short trip."

Crazy bastards.

"I'd rather get on the right side of this ladder."

"I'm here to make sure you do . . . eventually." He clamped a hand on my leg.

I wasn't going anywhere even if I had to let go with my hands.

Because these guys wouldn't let me down.

I swung my other leg up. Burke held it tight until the ladder was just above the deck of the truck.

"Let go," I said.

"Hang on a sec."

Walsh and Rivera supported my back, and Burke released my legs when he was sure they had me.

"Thanks." I took off in a desperate search for Pepper. There were two ambulances. Lincoln and Beau had the dogs from downstairs corralled. *What are they doing here?*

I didn't care. I was just grateful they were.

I fought my way through the small crowd to a stretcher. The doors to the ambulance beside it closed.

Pepper was lifeless, covered in soot. It was too dark to see if she was breathing.

I threw off my mask and leaned over her.

"Sir, we have to get her to the hospital." One of the paramedics I'd seen before calmed me with his hand on my shoulder.

"How bad is it?"

He didn't answer.

"I'm going."

"Only family allowed."

"I am her family," I growled as they put her in the ambulance.

"Sorry, sir, I need to take her now." Damn it.

The dogs.

Ash, Muffy, and Sadie.

I needed to make sure the dogs were okay.

"Take care of her," I said gruffly, allowing them to close the back doors.

Helplessly, I watched them take off with sirens blaring, torn in three directions. Those two women would want me here.

Since most of the dogs were okay in my siblings' care, I looked for the three in the worst shape. Ash had barely been breathing. Muffy and Sadie weren't much better.

I had to get them to Dr. Lyons.

"Did you drive?" I asked Lincoln.

"No. Are you okay?"

"Not really."

"Pepper and Miss Adeline?" Beau's voice cracked.

"I don't know." I frantically looked for the three dogs when I spotted them near Captain Koker's car.

A familiar black sedan rolled up to the scene. Dread filled me, even though that was a change from the others. Usually it was driving away.

I sprinted to the dogs.

My father's car stopped beside Captain Koker's. I picked up Ash and banged on the door with my foot.

It opened.

My father sat in the back with a suit on as if he hadn't suffered a heart attack days before.

"I need a ride."

Carefully, I lay Ash, Muffy, and Sadie inside. I tossed my oxygen tank, jumped in the front seat, and barked out Dr. Lyons's address.

"First day back and you're almost killed."

"Save it," I snapped.

"I warned you this would happen." *Not now, you ass.*

I unbuttoned my fire jacket and whipped around. "Because you *knew* it would?"

"Yes."

My worst fears felt confirmed. Was my own father trying to kill me too?

"Drive faster."

I didn't know the man behind the wheel, but he did as I asked, weaving through traffic as if he were a professional.

"I need your phone." I held out my hand to my father.

Slowly, my wits were coming back to me, though I was still a wreck.

He dropped it in my palm without hesitation. I scrolled through the contacts until I found my brother's name.

"Yeah."

I was surprised by Lincoln's annoyed answer. He played the game, pretending to respect our father. At least, I thought he did.

"Lincoln."

"Teague?"

"Can you take the dogs to Elliotts' place? He has the others." I sounded more in command and less uncertain than I actually felt.

"I'll see to it."

"Will you stay with them until I can get there?"

He was busy. That was a big ask considering I didn't know how long it would be. I liked the Elliotts. Pepper trusted them with their dogs.

But I trusted my brother more.

"Of course."

"If Burke is still around, get his phone number. Have him find out what hospital Pepper and Miss Adeline are in." She needed me. Hell, I needed her. But I was sure this was what she'd want me to do.

She'd never forgive me if I didn't do all I could for these three.

"Where can I contact you?" His unflappable voice soothed me.

"I'll be at Dr. Lyons's office with Sadie, Muffy, and Ash until I get the prognosis."

"And Dad is taking you?" he asked carefully. Hell had frozen over twice in one week.

"Yes." I switched ears.

"Why the hell was he there?"

"I have no idea. You ask him." I took another angry breath. "Get the dogs to the Elliotts, and tell Beau to go to the hospital. Miss Adeline and Pepper need family around. I'll be there when I can."

The irony wasn't lost on me that I'd hustled to the hospital when I'd gotten the news about my father, and I'd stayed by his side until he was released. And I hated the man.

The woman I loved had been taken away in an ambulance, one I should've been in with her, and I'd left her alone.

It wouldn't be for long.

I twisted around and touched Ash's head. She was still breathing . . . barely.

"Anything else?"

"Not for now. My phone is at the station, but I'll check in when I can." I pulled the phone away from my ear.

"Teague?"

I pressed it back to my face when Lincoln called my name. "Yeah?"

"I love you."

I swallowed hard. I knew he did. He showed me by being there for me, being my support. My rock. My best friend. I couldn't remember the last time he'd said that. But hell, did I need to hear that right now.

"Love you too."

I hung up and offered the phone to my father, who was ashen.

The driver pulled to the curb in front of the vet's office.

"Help me carry them inside?" I asked as I opened the car door.

My father moved to pick up Sadie, but I stopped him. "You can't lift heavy things."

He snarled but stayed put. The driver lifted Muffy. I grabbed Ash and burst into the clinic.

The technician behind the reception desk rushed to open the door to the back. "This way."

I deposited Ash on an exam table and ran to get Sadie. My father held the door to Dr. Lyons's office. I shoved down my shock and hurried to get her to the exam room.

Dr. Lyons already had a stethoscope against Ash.

"How are they, doc?" Gently, I lay Sadie down.

The driver backed out of the room.

"Put her in the oxygen chamber."

I lifted Ash before the vet tech could. She led me to another room lined with kennels and opened one with a glass door.

Dr. Lyons was right behind me with Muffy and deposited him in a similar kennel.

"We don't have another chamber."

I got Sadie and placed her on a table where the vet directed. She hooked a mask around the dog's muzzle and pressed buttons on a nearby machine.

That stubborn dog had led me to the others. She'd saved them. And she better not give up on me.

I'd give anything to hear that shrill bark demanding breakfast or any other B-word that came to mind.

I moved to Ash and touched the glass door that separated us. Poor girl. She'd survived one fire. Her lungs probably still hadn't fully healed from that.

But she was a fighter.

My fighter.

It was terrifying seeing these lively creatures unmoving.

Dr. Lyons steered me away from them and spoke quietly as if she didn't want them to hear what she had to say.

"I'm sorry, Teague. But they're in trouble."

CHAPTER FORTY-FOUR

PEPPER

BEEP. *Beep. Beep.*

I reached beside me, blindly trying to turn off my alarm. My hand hit something unfamiliar. I struggled to open my eyes.

My nose burned like I'd been standing over a fire, inhaling smoke for hours.

I jolted.

Fire.

The last thing I remembered was Miss Adeline passed out. *Oh no.* Had I passed out too?

It had been so hot. Was the fire out?

Open your eyes, Pepper.

I forced myself to fight past the sting. White light blinded me as I blinked to adjust.

"Are you awake, Pepper?" I recognized the voice but couldn't quite place it.

Everything was fuzzy.

I tried to lift my head. It was too heavy, so I lolled it to the side.

"Beau?"

"Oh thank God." She flung her arms around me and kissed my cheek. "Miss Adeline, she's awake."

Where were we? And of course, the old woman was fine. She was a tough old bird.

Instead of a snarky remark, silence was the only response.

"Is she—the dogs?" I couldn't make my mouth say the words in my head. And why was my voice muffled?

"She's right here. I had the doctors put you in the same room." Beau squeezed my hand. "The dogs are at Daniel and Vivian's."

Some of the pressure inside me released. "They're all okay?" My throat hurt. It was painful to speak.

She dropped her gaze. "Teague is with a few of them at the vet."

Teague.

A longing tugged at me. I'd barely seen him over the past week and as much as I appreciated Beau's presence, I wanted him.

"He thought you'd rather have him make sure they were okay before he came here."

He was right.

"So everyone is fine?"

She fiddled with the long gold chain dangling from her neck. "They will be," she said quietly.

I attempted to sit up. It was as if all my limbs weighed a thousand pounds. "How long have I been here?" There were wires hooked to me as if they were permanent fixtures.

Could I breathe on my own?

It occurred to me I had an oxygen mask over my face. I felt strange but not like I should be in a hospital.

Hospital.

Two visits in a matter of days when I'd never set foot in one before.

So dizzy. My head lolled again.

Beau jolted. "I'll get the nurse. Then call Teague."

She released my hand and rushed away.

I had a clear path to see Miss Adeline. Her machine beeped in a steady rhythm as mine did. I watched her still form under the thin sheet.

Her chest rose and fell. I took a full breath, not realizing I'd been holding it while I waited for movement.

She wasn't young.

It was easy to forget that sometimes when she had more energy and spunk than I did. I never considered her to be vulnerable, but she was.

"Wake up, woman."

"I am, since nobody around here lets anyone get any rest."

Tears leaked from the corners of my eyes at that sharp tongue.

"Have you seen the doctor yet? He's pretty handsome," I said.

"Pssh. I'm still mad that the one time I'm rescued by a hot fireman, I missed it." A coughing fit ensued.

The little relief I felt was replaced with worry.

"You scared me," I said when she'd settled.

"Just had to make sure you'd realize how much you love me." She grinned, but it was covered by her oxygen mask.

A nurse entered, followed by Beau.

"You're both awake." Beau beamed and glided over to Miss Adeline.

"Don't mention that," I muttered before she could go into another spiel about how she'd been up this whole time.

The nurse took both of our vitals, asked us a few questions, and promised a doctor would be by shortly.

"When can we get out of this place?" Miss Adeline asked.

For a second, I thought she was going to rip wires from her arms.

"What's your hurry? My guess is we don't have anywhere to go." My tone was light, but the pain in my chest was real.

"I'm so sorry, Pepper," Beau whispered. "You can stay at Lincoln's. I'm pretty sure Teague's loft is gone too. Or maybe I'll buy an apartment and you can move in with me." Beau flopped down in the chair she'd positioned between the beds.

"You're staying in New York?" I asked incredulously. I'd always had the impression she'd rather walk barefoot over hot coals than that.

She shrugged noncommittally. "It's just an idea."

"Good thing we had a plan B." Miss Adeline's tone didn't have quite the spark it usually did. She must be heartbroken to lose the place she'd built with her husband.

Plan B. Reminded me of B-words.

Sadie.

I couldn't remember where I'd seen her last. I'd give anything to hear her boss us around. What if—if the worst had happened? Would Beau tell me or wait?

"Sadie," I said hoarsely.

"She's with Dr. Lyons."

I jerked my head toward the door. Teague filled it, still in the pants and suspenders of his fire suit. He was filthy. His hair was all over the place. He looked like a mix between having no sleep and IV-ing energy drinks.

He touched Miss Adeline's foot as he passed but made a beeline for me. When he reached the side of the bed, he gripped the rail.

"I love you."

My eyes stung again, this time with more tears. Those words meant so much, especially now.

"I-I didn't tell you that when I found you in the fire." He sounded anguished.

I summoned all my strength and reached for his hand. "I probably wouldn't have heard you anyway."

"Not funny." He exhaled deeply and bent to kiss my forehead. "You okay?" He looked at Miss Adeline too.

"Just waiting on this supposed hot doctor to get me out of here," she said.

"She's fine," I said with a smile. "How are the dogs?"

He hesitated. "Sadie, I don't know how she breathed in so much smoke and still managed to find me. She led me to the four of you."

I nearly choked on the knot in my throat. That girl seemed like we annoyed her most of the time. Like we were there to serve her. But she loved hard.

"She and Ash and Muffy"—he swallowed—"they're . . ." He closed his eyes. "They have to make it," he whispered.

"I need to see them." I threw off my covers and tried to scoot off the bed.

"You need to recover. Dr. Lyons is taking good care of them. Lincoln is with the others at the Elliotts'. Everyone is going to be okay."

I wasn't sure if he was trying to convince me or himself. But Teague didn't make empty promises.

"Thank you," I said as he covered me up again. "You saved us."

"How'd the fire start?" He brushed off any thanks, though I hadn't expected any different. It was who he was.

"I don't know." I flitted through my memories from the evening before. "I'd put most of the dogs downstairs to get ready for supper. The fire inspector came by—"

"Fire inspector?" Teague asked sharply.

"Yeah. They come by every so often." That was nothing unusual. The time was a little strange, but I figured they were overloaded with work.

"Who was it?"

I tried to think. I was so tired. Everything was a struggle. "I'm not sure he said. I-I can't remember."

Teague brushed the hair back from my face. "That's okay. Do you feel up to telling me what happened next?"

I closed my eyes, looking back at the rescue.

"He needed to see upstairs. Miss Adeline and those three hadn't come down. I warned him about the dogs. He suggested I close us all in a room while he looked around. That it wouldn't take long."

If he hadn't said it, I would have. The dogs were sweet and generally well-behaved, but I never knew how they'd react to strangers. They'd been happy to have more time with us in my room.

"Sadie started barking from the other side of the door. I thought she wanted her supper."

"Then we smelled smoke," Miss Adeline said.

"We couldn't get the door to my room open." I'd yanked and tugged. I even tried to find a screwdriver in my drawers to no avail.

"The inspector didn't help you?" Teague made a valiant effort to keep his voice neutral but failed to mask his anger. Had the inspector blocked the door somehow?

"We yelled—"

"He never answered," Miss Adeline finished.

"The smoke got so bad so quickly. I couldn't remember if I should open a window or not, so I did." Had that been the wrong thing to do? Short of breaking down the door, I hadn't seen another option.

"It's best not to because oxygen fuels the fire. But it was your only way out so you did the right thing."

He eased my unspoken fears that I'd made the situation worse. "Hopefully I won't need to remember again." I never wanted to go through another fire again.

"Would you be able to identify the inspector if you saw him?" Teague asked with the respect of someone who had been through a situation like this before.

He made the whole thing so much easier than if he weren't here.

"I think so."

He kissed my forehead again. "Rest now. And don't worry. Everything will be fine."

"Always is," Miss Adeline said as if she hadn't just lost all her worldly possessions.

It didn't matter. We had what was most important.

I removed my oxygen mask. Teague tried to stop me, but I swatted his hand and crooked my finger. He leaned close. He smelled like smoke and home.

I brushed my lips against his. He saved my life. Our lives. I couldn't live without this man, and he needed to know that. "I love you."

CHAPTER FORTY-FIVE

TEAGUE

"YOU DIDN'T HAVE to go to these lengths to get us in a fancy apartment."

Pepper elbowed Miss Adeline in the side.

"I heard that," Vivian said as she straightened the table of dog treats for humans.

Pepper blushed. I hid my smile.

Vivian had suggested postponing the fundraiser, but these two had insisted it go on. Pepper's exact words had been "get it over with" because she knew many of the dogs would be adopted as a result of the event. It had been nine days since the fire, and even though the doctor had ordered bed rest for both of them, they were here. Upright. Caring for their dogs. I'd never known anyone, let alone two hard-headed women, take such care for dogs before. She amazed me. They both did really.

"It worked, didn't it?" Miss Adeline elbowed her back. "But you blew us shacking up with another handsome man."

Pepper rolled her eyes.

Lincoln had insisted we all stay at his place, but Daniel and Vivian had offered one of the empty apartments in their building. Pepper felt it was best to go there because most of the dogs were already there and they had room for more.

Lincoln would've gladly transformed the basketball court, but Pepper was right.

They'd gone straight from the hospital to a new home, and we'd all adjusted well.

Daniel shook my hand. "Were you able to salvage anything?"

My loft had been a casualty of the fire too. I'd had visions of knocking down the wall between the two apartments but not like that.

"A few things. The most important ones." I pointed to Pepper and Miss Adeline.

They hadn't made any decisions on what they were going to do with the destroyed property yet. Daniel and Vivian were kind enough to give them all the time they needed to figure it out.

"We're going to get these babies a ton of money today." Vivian looped her arm through her husband's. "Aren't we?"

"I assume we're both writing a check," he said dryly.

She bumped his hip. "Ding. Ding. Ding."

Pepper shifted uncomfortably. She had a hard time taking help or money from anyone. Though she was learning to, it still wasn't easy for her.

Ash pawed my leg. I stooped and she rolled over. "You want a belly rub?"

By a miracle, she'd recovered from smoke inhalation twice. And now that I had expert help, she was mine. Well, ours. But she always had been. It just took me longer to realize that.

Sadie and Muffy crept to the buffet table. They sniffed and looked around innocently. Pepper watched with amused hawk eyes.

Muffy put his head on the table. Sadie went for it, snagging a treat Garrison had crafted. The towering display toppled.

It rained treats on their heads. Muffy gobbled up as many as he could like a vacuum.

"Sadie," Pepper scolded before she covered her mouth.

These two were up to their old ways like they'd never missed a beat. Dr. Lyons hadn't been confident they'd make it through the first twenty-four hours, but somehow, they'd fought for their lives. After a few more days, Sadie had caused so much trouble at Dr. Lyons's office they'd given her a going away party when she'd recovered.

"Told you the guests would love them," Vivian called to Garrison.

"I won't doubt you again." He opened a fresh box of treats and replaced the missing ones.

People piled into the park.

Pepper chewed on her lip.

I slung an arm around her shoulder. "We don't have to adopt out anyone if you don't want to."

She leaned into me. "I know."

She'd confessed how she felt, and I now completely understood. These dogs were our family. We had to think about what was best for them. Letting them go, even to loving families, was hard.

"Are we late?" Beau rushed over and threw her arms around both of us.

Lincoln was close behind without Beau's urgency. "So far, I like this fundraiser better than the others." He had on a suit and was completely overdressed.

Daniel also had on a suit, though he'd ditched the tie.

I didn't like charity events much either. Most were stuffy and pretentious. Vivian and Muriella had done a great job of creating a celebratory atmosphere.

Because we were celebrating. Everyone was okay.

"How'd you get the afternoon off?" Beau punched me in the arm.

"Told all the guys they could come too."

The captain had been none too pleased about that, but the dayshift crew had been happy to stay over a few hours today.

"Yo. Hollingsworth."

Right on cue, my boys showed up.

"Yo." I waved them over.

"We invited some of the other stations. Hope that's okay," Burke said.

"Thank you." Pepper hugged him long and hard.

The fire had bonded all of us in a way we hadn't been before. We'd survived tragedy. And this man had saved each and every one of us. He was one of the best men I knew, and I'd never forget what he did for my family. My girls.

"There she is." Burke picked up Miss Adeline and twirled her around.

"You know my bones are fragile," she said.

"Ain't nothing delicate about you."

She winked. "Damn straight."

Beau scowled at Cal like she'd been taking lessons from Lincoln. Across the way, another group of guys and girls from other fire stations crossed the grass. Cal led the pack in long strides.

What was her deal when it came to him?

He said hello to everyone but her. I opened my mouth to ask my sister what I was missing, but Burke pulled me and Pepper aside.

"Willa talked to the investigators working the fire at Grey Paws," he said in a hushed voice. "They have an ignition point."

"Where did it start?" Pepper asked.

"The grill."

What? We hadn't used it in days. I was pretty sure the ladies hadn't. "How?"

"We hadn't used it. That's impossible."

Burke held up his hands. "I only know what I'm told, but it makes sense. The fire was worse upstairs than the bottom floor initially."

"They think it was an accident or intentional?" I held Pepper's hand. She didn't need my support. I needed hers.

"She didn't say."

I cocked my head. "You never told me who the suspect in the other fires is."

Pepper shielded her eyes from the sun. "That's him."

"How do you know?" Burke asked.

"That's the fire inspector," Pepper said insistently.

Captain Koker walked to the edge of the grass . . . with my father. *What the hell is he doing here?*

"Did Willa tell you?" Burke pressed.

She shook her head. "Tell me what?"

"Koker's prints are at every scene."

I rubbed my face as my mind whirled. "Why wouldn't they be? He's the captain."

"None of ours are."

"We wear gloves," I argued.

"And they're from like before the fires started." Burke raised his voice.

With the technology at the investigation unit, they could determine facts that seemed impossible.

I didn't like the man, but it seemed like a stretch to blame him.

"Who *is* he?" Pepper pointed her chin.

"That's Captain Koker. The one who fired me," I said through my teeth.

"Does he usually do inspections?"

Burke and I looked at one another and answered simultaneously. "No."

Images from the fire came back to me. "There was a dresser in front of your door." I spoke in disbelief. I'd registered that as strange at the time but had forgotten when my focus had been on getting everyone to safety.

"You never told me that," Pepper said.

"I just thought of it."

"Why would he pose as an inspector when he's not?" she asked slowly.

"He'd just found out you were back on at the station. Chief went over his head."

Had he had time to get to Pepper's? I didn't doubt her, but the day was a blur.

"So what? He retaliated by setting Grey Paws on fire?"

He'd never liked me. It wasn't a secret. Firing me was one thing. Attempted murder was another.

"He nearly killed you." I didn't recognize my own voice. It was feral.

Before I could think, my feet were moving.

He nearly killed her. Killed them.

Lincoln would tell me to build a solid case and nail him. And he would probably be right.

But I didn't have time to do that.

I'd already tried and convicted him in my mind.

I reared back and landed a blow to his face so hard he fell to the ground. The crowded park went silent as I stood over him with my foot on his chest.

"I want to hear it," I hissed.

"You're fired." He smirked.

I applied more pressure to his chest, and it quickly faded.

"Chief promote you to fire inspector?" I flexed my fist, itching to land another hit.

Koker's eyes flared, but there wasn't a single ounce of regret in them.

"Hollingsworth!" Burke yelled.

I felt a swarm behind me, but my focus was solely on this murdering sack of garbage.

A hand landed on my shoulder. Then another.

"Think about this," Walsh said. "You'll be done."

I didn't care. I wanted Koker done.

"Tell. Me." The demand was harsh. Anger like I'd never felt erupted. I stomped on his stomach.

"Ugh." He tried to curl up in pain, but I made him take it.

That was nothing compared to finding Pepper, Miss Adeline, and the dogs surrounded by fire and nearly dead.

"Teague." Pepper appeared, standing near Koker's head. She wasn't telling me to stop or go. Just to think. And whatever I decided, she was behind me.

The calm in the chaos.

"I'm not moving until he's arrested."

She nodded. He'd almost taken her away from me. I didn't want him to rot in jail. I wanted to kill him. But I wouldn't let him ruin the life I was building with Pepper.

That didn't mean I couldn't hit him again for good measure.

I kicked him in the ribs. It wasn't enough. My grasp on control was slipping.

He nearly killed Pepper.

This SOB was going to jail in pain.

My father tilted his head, catching my eye. He wore his ever-present stone-like expression. Why was he here? And with this jackass? Maybe they were working together and Koker had given him a heart attack too.

I had no proof Koker was responsible for the others beside the fingerprints. But I was damn sure he'd set Pepper and Miss Adeline's apartment on fire.

My father flashed his version of triumph as I drew back my fist.

"Are you sure you want to decimate your uncle?"

CHAPTER FORTY-SIX

PEPPER

TEAGUE'S ARM WENT LIMP.

"What the hell are you talking about?" Beau planted a hand on her hip. She hardly spared a glance to the man on the ground. Her focus was lasered on her father.

Not only was I stunned that Teague's boss was his uncle but also that their father would air their personal business in such a public way.

Lincoln remained quiet.

Teague stared at the man under his boot as if he'd never seen him before.

How many more blows did he have to take? He'd been through enough. We were finding our peace and starting a new path. He deserved some happiness.

"Food and cute dogs this way." Vivian steered the crowd like a professional herder until the only people left besides Miss Adeline and me were Hollingsworths.

"Impossible. You're an only child and Mom's brother never came back from boarding school," Teague said.

"And he's returned," his father said smoothly.

"You knew all along."

Samuel Hollingsworth put his hands in his pockets. "Not until the fires started. It took me a lot of years to discover his true identity."

"Talk faster." Teague glared at his father's casual stance.

"I never met Morgan. I only knew what your mother told me about him, which wasn't much." He flicked his gaze toward the man on the ground. "He always had a penchant for fire. He burned your grandparents' home to the ground when he was twelve."

"No one ever proved that," Koker wheezed.

"Be quiet, Morgan." A flash of annoyance colored his father's face. "They shipped him to military school, hoping to discipline him." He waved his hand in disgust. "Obviously a waste of time and effort."

"Mom's maiden name wasn't Koker," Beau said.

"The rash of fires went from California to Florida and in between as your grandparents' shuffled him from school to school. Eventually, they had to give him a new identity."

Teague's foot remained on his uncle's chest. "Why isn't he in jail?"

"It's no secret your mother's family was worth a fortune. If you're willing to pay, anything can go away." His father lifted a brow.

"How are you involved with him?" Teague balled his fist.

Lincoln noticed but remained silent.

"He has . . . financial difficulties. You know better than I do what a meager wage a fireman makes." The dig seemed to bounce off Teague. "I want you out of that job. For a price, he was willing to ensure that happened."

"He's been my supervisor for years," Teague said.

His father sighed. "Apparently, the chief is willing to overlook your transgressions and isn't so easily bought."

"You tried to destroyed my career." Teague threw his hands up. "People have been killed. Pepper and Miss Adeline nearly were." His voice reached a crescendo that drew the attention of nearby people.

"You're foolish, bullheaded, and impossible to reason with." His father rattled off a list of characteristics like he'd thought of them so often they were ingrained in his mind.

What the hell?

"He tried to murder the woman I love," Teague yelled. I'd never seen him so angry.

His father just glared. Bastard.

Blue lights flashed. Sirens wailed.

A fleet of New York Police Department cars skidded to a stop beside us.

"Yo. He's right there." Burke pointed to Koker . . . or whoever he was. "I called them." He jerked his head toward the police.

"Move your foot, sir."

As if he didn't realize he was still standing on the man, he reluctantly lifted it.

"Willa's going to turn over the evidence they have on him in connection to the other fires. Pepper's an eyewitness in their fire." Burke folded his arms.

"Hope it's enough to put him away for a long time."

Burke nodded and stalked over to Walsh and Rivera.

"He'll be released." Teague's father spoke quietly but certainly.

"Let me guess. You'll see to it," Teague said bitterly.

He didn't answer.

How could his father ensure that? His power must have no limit even for the law. Not even murder.

"He deserves hellfire and brimstone for what he did." Teague stared at the squad car until it disappeared.

"We've finally found something we agree upon." He strode toward the river.

"Wait." I jogged toward him. "Do you know why he killed my parents and aunt?"

Samuel Hollingsworth was the only one who seemed to have any solid leads. *I* didn't have any connections to Koker.

He studied me for a moment. "It's difficult to know the inner workings of an insane person's mind, but my assumption is in retaliation for Teague."

"I didn't know he was my uncle. Why would he have it out for me?" Teague was at my back, right there to support me.

His father checked his watch. "Money. It's always about money."

"You just said Teague makes a *meager* salary." I put the word in air quotes.

He stared at his son. "He has an inheritance. One I can only suppose Morgan feels rightfully belongs to him."

"Don't Beau and Lincoln have one too?" I asked. I didn't know how rich people determined who got what, but what little I knew of Teague's mother, she wouldn't give more to one child than another.

"They do." He put his hand back into his pocket. "Their mother labored over which child would get what assets. She wanted them to be suited to their interests and attributes. When she set up the trusts, the values were equal. She couldn't have predicted the assets in Teague's would skyrocket in value." He looked at Beau and Lincoln. "He's lucky his siblings aren't the greedy, jealous type."

Teague appeared appalled. "I didn't—I thought we all had the same," he said apologetically.

"I've never touched my trust," Beau said, lifting one shoulder and lowering it. "And he has more money than all of us put together." She pointed a thumb at Lincoln.

"You think I'm a terrible father, but I did something right."

Teague stared at his father.

"How is killing my aunt and parents retaliation against Teague?" I couldn't wrap my mind around all these horrible events.

"I told you I don't know," he said impatiently. "Maybe he didn't want Teague to have money or love. Maybe he hoped to scare all of you into doing whatever it is he wanted."

He spoke in possibilities but sounded certain in his answer. It was all so ugly.

"I must go." He tilted his head. "I underestimated you, Pepper. You hired shark attorneys, but I'll have that small-time attorney toss that letter."

"You were behind that?" Teague growled.

"I capitalized on an opportunity," his father said. "I need you at Hollingsworth Properties. She's the only one who seems to motivate you."

He vanished into the distance. A silence descended on us.

"I feel like I've been slapped." Beau rubbed her cheek for emphasis.

"I need a piece of cake." Miss Adeline had been unusually quiet.

"Let's go." Beau linked arms with her.

"You okay? That was a lot to take in." I put an arm around Teague's waist. I still hadn't figured out if his father was involved in the fires. Apparently the authorities didn't think so since he didn't so much as have to answer a single question.

We looked at the partygoers who seemed to have already forgotten the drama. Laughter floated toward the sky. Dogs barked and chased each other.

"Yeah," he said slowly. "I just . . . I'm just so sorry, Pepper. I brought all of this on you, Miss Adeline, and—"

"Stop, Teague. You can't blame yourself here."

"No, I can. Well, I can't take responsibility for the crazy that is my family. I'm just so angry. You, Miss Adeline, all the dogs. You could have been killed."

"But I wasn't. We're okay. The dogs all survived. Someone was looking after us that day." I had to believe in that to not relive the terrifying moments of being locked in that room with the smoke and fire and fear of death. Teague shook his head.

"I love you."

"I love you too. Think the trouble is over?"

He kissed the side of my head. "Sadie isn't going anywhere, so I'd say that's a definite no."

I grinned. "Trouble is here to stay."

CHAPTER FORTY-SEVEN

TEAGUE

"ARE WE REALLY DOING THIS?"

Pepper dragged her feet as we approached the iron gate. I didn't blame her. The last time we'd been here hadn't been pleasant.

It wasn't my favorite place either.

"I need answers."

She put her hand over mine as I lifted the latch. "We don't know that we'll get them."

And what she didn't say was that all this turmoil and heartache could be for nothing.

"It's a risk I'm willing to take."

She lifted her hand, a silent acceptance that she supported my decision. It was one of the many things I loved most about her. She let me be who I was . . . and was right with me, even when I was still figuring things out.

I rang the doorbell. Jitters I rarely felt skittered through me. *I hope this is the right move.*

Pepper tapped her foot while we waited. "Miss Adeline is going to want a full rundown when we get home. I hope we have more to tell her than we waited an hour for the door to be answered."

I snickered, grateful she had a sense of humor no matter the situation.

"You're late." Winston threw open the door with a scowl for the ages. I thought Lincoln had learned that from our father, but maybe I was wrong.

I shucked his shoulder. "Not the first time and won't be the last."

"I raised you better than that," he said as he stepped aside.

"You did." I hugged him despite the fact we weren't usually affectionate. To my surprise, he hugged me back.

"I'm glad to see you." He spoke quietly in my ear. There was an undertone of emotion and a wave of regret crashed over me.

"Let's not be strangers anymore."

"I'll hold you to that." He led us through the foyer to the formal dining room. "He's not pleased with your tardiness."

Is my father ever pleased? He should be happy I'd contacted him at all.

"I thought it was just going to be the three of us," Pepper whispered as she took in the twenty-seat dining table in the monstrous room.

"Plus him." I pointed to the bust on a pedestal of a man whose identity I wasn't even sure of. Somebody from Mom's side of the family, I supposed.

Pepper appeared a little overwhelmed at the ostentatiousness of the dining room. I pulled out the chair next to the one that used to be mine. We'd only eaten in here on holidays.

"My mom thought this room was absurd too," I said once we'd sat.

That seemed to relax her a fraction.

"What about them?" Her eyes widened as she took in the portraits of my ancestors that lined the walls.

"Lincoln used to try to convince Beau and me that our great grandfather's eyes move." I pointed to him.

Pepper shuddered even as she stared.

"Your mother told him that."

She startled at the sound of my father's voice. He was a phantom, just like the people on these walls.

I hadn't figured out if he dropped these little nuggets about her to hurt me or if it was because she was constantly on his mind. There was a time I wouldn't have thought that possible. Now, I wasn't so sure.

He stood at the head of the table, just as he'd done all my life, and surveyed its length.

"Why do you do that?" I assumed it was to prove he was lord and master of this domain.

"Because your grandfather did before all of our family meals."

I'd have to hand it to my father. He seemed to be all about the family traditions. Unfortunately, I must have come from a long line of stuffy and unfeeling jerks on his side.

"I never did thank you," Pepper said once he'd taken his seat. *What did she possibly have to thank him for?* "Teague told me you rushed Sadie, Muffy, and Ash to Dr. Lyons after the fire. I wouldn't have expected that from you. But I'm grateful."

His brow furrowed. I placed a hand on her knee, beyond amazed at her bravery. Not many people would have the courage to speak their mind to him. I certainly hadn't much over the years.

He grunted and appeared unsure. I'd never seen that before.

Winston entered with a serving tray of steaming soup in fine china bowls. I regretted he wouldn't join us since he'd been more of a father to me than my own. It didn't seem right to have him serve us, but that was the place he liked.

Pepper fiddled with the two choices of spoons and finally settled on a smaller one.

My father unfolded his napkin with a flourish and placed it on his lap.

"How were you involved in the fires and murders?" I hadn't come here to share a meal. I wanted answers. My stomach was too turbulent to eat anyway.

"Can we not enjoy a meal before the interrogation?" He spooned the soup into his mouth noiselessly.

I pushed mine away. "*You* insisted on dinner. Not me."

"Our time together is always so hostile." He continued to eat, as if what I wanted was meaningless.

"Any guesses as to why?"

Pepper sipped her water and glanced at me to see if I was okay. No. I was not. We hadn't been here five minutes and my blood was close to a raging boil. My father was pretending to be pleasant to get a rise out of me.

And it was working.

I should be better than this.

"Why did you buy the building next door to Grey Paws?" She took a bite of soup, obviously much better at playing his game than I was. Pepper gave him what he wanted—sharing a meal—while going after what she wanted—answers.

I still felt duped that he'd been my landlord. What a fool he must take me for.

"Believe or not, the surrounding area is quite desirable now. It's only a matter of time before the property values on that street skyrocket."

"You don't know that," I said petulantly.

He barely looked up. "Son, I've been around real estate my entire life. I know trends better than anyone else in this city. I have the fortune to prove it."

I hated that he was behaving as if we were a normal family having a nice dinner. This wasn't what I'd intended when I'd called to set up a meeting. I'd planned to spend as little time together as possible, fairly certain I'd leave with more questions than answers.

But I had to try.

"How did you get me to move in there?" I asked. Obviously, he'd been following me, but getting me to make maneuvers without direct contact? He was good.

"I had Morgan put up the flyer at the fire station." He spoke evenly, as if he'd done nothing out of the ordinary.

"You had no way of knowing I'd take it." I folded my arms over my chest.

"Your lease was up. The building suits your simple style." He smirked. "You took it, didn't you?"

I pressed my foot into the table leg so hard it moved an inch. "Why do you follow me?"

His expression turned hard. "I watch all my children."

"*Why?*"

"To make sure you don't suffer the same fate as your mother." I dropped my arms and my jaw.

Pepper reached for my hand.

I pointed at him. "You don't get to do that. You don't get to pretend like you care."

"I've no idea where you got the impression I don't care." His spoon clinked in the bowl.

"From you," I shouted.

My heartbeat pounded so loud in my ears I though my eardrums would explode. I'd known this wouldn't be easy when I walked into the house, but I wasn't prepared for this.

My chair scraped as I stood. "You have tried to destroy my life at every turn—"

"Wanting what's best for you isn't destruction."

How dare he continue to spout his lies. I gripped the back of Pepper's chair.

"That job is beneath you. And more than that, it's dangerous," he continued, as if my thoughts didn't matter. Because they didn't to him.

"And yet you colluded with this supposed uncle of mine, which nearly killed Pepper, Miss Adeline, the dogs, and me? Give me a break." I threw my hands up.

"I had nothing to do with those fires or murders." He remained calm, which only amped up my anger.

How could he be so emotionless?

"You were at every scene," I shouted. "Who were those people at the fire Cassano was injured in?"

I'd never made their association, but they had to be related. Had to be.

He looked out the window.

Winston returned and removed our soup bowls. He gave me a silent nod of support.

When he disappeared, my father sighed. "Distant cousins of yours on your mother's side."

I sank back into my chair. "Did I know them?" After Mom died, we saw our grandparents and that was it. I had extended family, at least I'd assumed, but we had nothing to do with them.

"No. They received ten million of your grandparents' estate."

The amount was spoken so flippantly, as if everyone got that kind of inheritance.

Pepper balled her napkin in her fist.

Ash belonged to my family.

"I don't understand the purpose of murdering them." I dropped my chin to my chest. Guilt for their loss ate away at some of the anger.

"As I explained before, he felt he had been cheated out of what was rightfully his." He adjusted his tie. "I'm not sure that one was aimed so much at you as just revenge for what he perceived was stolen from him."

That made me feel only marginally better.

"He killed Cassano," I said in a low growl.

"Did he know Koker was responsible for that fire?" Pepper asked.

My father's face was an emotionless mask. "I don't know."

"You spent time with him. You have to know something." My voice rose.

"He's quite deceptive. Initially, my only interest in him was how he could be of use to get you out of that job."

I yanked on my hair. "Why do you want me at Hollingsworth Properties so badly?"

"I've already explained it to you."

I shook my head. "Not buying it. There's more to it than you want all your children working for your beloved company."

He scowled at Pepper. "If it weren't for your mother's fortune, the company would be defunct."

I rubbed the side of my face. "I thought you were the best."

"I am. At one time, it was my family's business. They made foolish decisions. I never wanted to use your mother's money, but I had no choice."

I couldn't imagine him ever being in financial peril. How humiliating to be forced to ask my mother to bail him out.

"But you're the only one from your family at the company," I said.

"Because I forced them out."

There was no regret in his expression. Had he left them destitute? I had no idea. This must have happened before I was born or when I was too young to understand.

I slumped in my chair. Pepper looked as exhausted by this zigzag of info as I was.

"This is what you need to know," my father said. "You will never have to be concerned about Morgan ever hurting anyone again."

I'd considered going to see him in prison. I wanted to understand why my uncle did the things he did. We'd worked together for so long. I knew him and yet he was a stranger. A stranger I was related to.

"And what about you?" Pepper asked. "Will you hurt us?"

His nostrils flared. "I will do what is best for my family."

"How were you at all those fire scenes? How did you know?" I spoke quietly. I didn't understand him. How he could kidnap Pepper and somehow pretend to care about me.

"Scanner."

Winston returned with the main course.

"I can't eat," I said.

"Try." Winston nudged my plate before he left again.

"If you continue to be a dog kicker, a kidnapper, and intimidator, we can't have anything to do with you."

I jerked my head toward Pepper. Was she considering forgiving him for all the horrors he'd done?

"I will leave your rescue alone . . . unless you give me a reason not to." My father cut into his porterhouse.

"What about Teague? Will you stop interfering in his life?"

He wiped his mouth and leveled her with his gaze. "Concern is not interference."

"It's creepy," she said. "He's a grown man."

"And I look after what's mine."

I stared at him. I'd never understand him. I needed to accept that.

"I didn't want it to be this way. I just wanted my dad." I leaned back in my chair.

He set down his knife and fork. "Everything I do is for you and your siblings. I don't expect you to understand. And I won't give up on you coming to your rightful place."

"Then don't expect to ever see me again."

I was done. He had some warped way of thinking. Whether his intentions were noble or not didn't matter. I couldn't do this anymore.

I stood and offered my hand to Pepper. She placed hers in mine and followed me to the door.

"I'm watching you, Son."

I hesitated but didn't turn around. That wasn't news. He was the way he was, and I couldn't change him.

I had to learn to live my way, his desires be damned.

"Well, that was . . . not the best." Pepper let out a breath as soon as we were outside.

"Do you think it sounds like he was trying to protect me?" I asked as I helped her in the truck.

"As much as I hate to say it, yeah. But that makes no sense." She lifted a shoulder and lowered it.

"I can't hold on to my hate." I put my forehead against hers.

"Good."

I snapped up. "You don't think I should?"

"No. I think we should love." She cupped my cheeks. "You're not the hateful type."

I grinned. "I'm not, am I?"

"Nope."

I gripped her thighs. "Thanks for doing this."

She brushed her lips across mine. "Anytime."

"Ready to go home?"

She beamed. "Let's go home."

EPILOGUE
TEAGUE

"DID your dog piss on my truck?"

Pepper grinned as Muffy put his leg down.

"We were washing it." I held up the soapy washcloth. "You owed me, but somehow I ended up doing it."

"Sounds fair to me." She scooped up some suds from the bucket and flicked them in my face.

Muffy jumped to catch them and failed miserably.

"Why you little—"

I chased Pepper, and she grabbed the hose.

"Watch how you finish that sentence." She aimed straight for my chest.

"Do it," Miss Adeline called from a nearby chair. "Wet T-shirt contest." She hooted, and I burst out laughing.

"New calendar proofs are in next week," I said.

"Get me two. I need to brag at the deli."

This was my life. Crazy chaos. Two women and a bunch of dogs that kept me entertained.

"If you get those calendars, I'm framing October and hanging it in the living room."

Pepper knew I despised posing, but it was for a good cause.

"I thought you'd take out a billboard," I pouted.

Water hit my chest. Pepper giggled and sprayed again. Muffy tried to get a drink, and Ash joined in. Sadie looked annoyed.

"Give me that." I lunged for Pepper.

She darted to the other side of the truck and aimed.

"I thought you were washing the truck today." Beau strolled down the sidewalk with Lincoln in tow.

"And we thought you were bringing lunch. I don't see anything that remotely looks like food," Miss Adeline said.

"Pizza's coming," Beau said. "Impatient much?"

"More like starving."

Woof.

Sadie stood.

"Does she know another S-word?" I asked.

"She knows the whole English language," Pepper said.

"How about *will you marry me*? Does she know that one?" I rested my arms on the side of the truck bed.

"I-I'm not sure." The hose went limp in Pepper's hands.

"Maybe if I get down on one knee? Would that help?" I rounded the truck and took the hose from her.

With her hand in mine, I led her to the sidewalk where we met. It had been four months since the fire, and Grey Paws had been demolished. Together we were planning our fresh start. And it seemed apt that my brother and sister were here for this moment. My family, altogether in one place. Safe.

I lowered to one knee. Ash, Muffy, and Sadie attacked me with licks and nudges, jockeying to be petted.

Pepper covered her mouth with her hand. Her eyes were bright and full of love as she looked down at me. "Yes."

"What was that? I can't hear you." I struggled to keep a straight face.

She dropped her hand. "I said *yes*."

I slipped a diamond on her left ring finger, and my world clicked into place. She was my beginning and end. My life. My calm. My forever home.

"I told you she'd say yes." Miss Adeline leaned back confidently.

"Did you know about this?" Pepper shook her finger at the old woman, who was now like a mother to both of us.

She buffed her nails. "Beats me."

An SUV stopped in the street.

"Pizza's here. Perfect timing," Beau said.

"We probably should have had something a little more . . . celebratory." I'd been so excited, I hadn't thought it through.

"It's perfect." Pepper pecked me on the mouth.

A man in a suit with a skinny tie stepped onto the sidewalk. "Lincoln Hollingsworth?"

My brother didn't move. "That's me."

The man lifted his dark aviator shades. "You're under arrest for securities fraud and tax evasion."

ENJOY THIS BOOK?

You can make a huge difference.

Reviews encourage other readers to try out a book. They are critically important to getting your favorite books in the hands of new readers.

We'd appreciate your help in spreading the word. If you could take a quick moment to leave a review on your favorite book site, we would be forever grateful. It can be as short as you like. You can do that on your favorite book retailer, Goodreads, and BookBub.

Email us (grahame@grahameclaire.com) a link to your review so we can be sure to thank you. Together, we can ensure our friends aren't left out.

Thank you so very much.

BOOK STUFF

The idea for Teague and Pepper's story started with our love of dogs. They truly are a best friend, a comfort, excellent listeners, and . . . sometime mischievous.

When that first scene in Crash made it to paper, we knew this would be a special story. But we had no idea it would turn into the adventure it did.

We were surprised many, many times along the way. Then again, with Miss Adeline's spunk, who could possibly know what she'd say next?

There are so many relationships we adored as the story unfolded. The way Teague and Pepper fit so well. Our favorite kind of love is one that neither hero nor heroine are looking for, but it hits them straight in the heart.

Miss Adeline and Pepper are quite the pair. Their banter made us laugh. Their teamwork tugged at our heartstrings. And their love of the dogs . . . well, it just added a depth of our connection to this world.

And then there's Teague, Lincoln, and Beau. We might've mentioned before that we do very little plotting when we write a story. They unfold themselves better than we could ever plan. So we didn't even know Lincoln and Beau existed until Teague introduced us.

They have such a special bond. One we never expected. And we can't wait to see what's ahead for them.

Some familiar favorites popped up too. We loved seeing Daniel, Vivian, M, Stone, Mrs. Quinn, and even Zegas and Whitley. Every time they show up it's like coming home. We hope you enjoy seeing them too.

We've completely fallen head over heels with this family and look forward to where they'll take us next.

xoxo,
Grahame Claire

ACKNOWLEDGMENTS

The process of how every book comes together is different each time. Sometimes life throws curve balls. The Crash & Burn duet definitely came together through the patience and flexibility of our team.

Our families endured a lot of late nights and early mornings while cheering us on. We can't ever thank them enough for their love and support.

Marion Archer, you took these books and made them into something special. You were flexible and understanding and we are so grateful for not only the magic you create, but your friendship.

Karen Lawson and Janet Hitchcock, we adore how you roll with everything without complaining. You are two of the loveliest people and it's an honor to work with you.

Lori Sabin, we're thrilled to have you as part of our team. You've made grammar fun. Thank you for your attention to detail and willingness to walk us through everything.

Alessandra Torre, we can't thank you enough for all the support and encouragement you've given us over the years.

Tia Louise, thank you for your kindness and for being such an inspiration.

P. Dangelico, thank you so much for your honesty and help along the way.

Claudia Burgoa, we're incredibly lucky to call you a friend. Thank you for always being there.

Catherine Cowles, no matter where we are in life, we can always count on you. Everyone should be lucky enough to have someone like you to call friend.

Emma Renshaw, so thankful for your friendship. You are one of the strongest people we know.

SueBee, where would we be without you? Thank you for your friendship and love.

Patricia Carlisle, your positivity is inspiring. We love your outlook on life and are so grateful for your friendship.

Belinda Graham, without you, this duet wouldn't have ever been finished. You always know when to send chocolate! Thank you for being such an amazing friend.

Wendy Ragan, there are some people that just connect and we're so glad we met you. Thank you for all the chats. Someday we will hug you in person.

Lara Petterson, thank you for all of your support and friendship. And the cookies. ;) We'll have a beach day soon.

The wonderful ladies of Grahame Claire Reader Hangout . . . we are so lucky to know each of you. We can't thank you enough for all you do.

Our beta readers Jessica, Christy, Diane, L. Duarte, Sonia, and Sabrina . . . you are so critical to our books. Thank you for your time and your friendship.

To the dogs we've loved and lost, we wouldn't be who we are without your unconditional love.

And to you, the best readers in the whole world, thank you for loving our stories and characters as much as we do. You inspire us, and we appreciate you more than we'll ever be able to express.

ALSO BY GRAHAME CLAIRE

ABOUT THE AUTHOR

Grahame Claire is a *USA Today* bestselling author of contemporary romance.

A writer. A blogger. United by our love of stories and all things romance. There was definitely some insta-love. Hello? Books involved. A little courting. A lot of writing. The result . . . Grahame Claire.

Soulmates. Unashamed of our multiple book boyfriends. Especially the ones that rooted in our heads and wouldn't leave us alone. Don't worry. We'll share.

Pleased to meet you.

Our favorite thing about being an author is you, the reader. So please, reach out. If you want to get on the exclusive mailing list (trust us, you do), you can do that at www.grahameclaire.com/newsletter.

Let's chat books on Goodreads. We can gossip about our book boyfriends on Twitter at @grahamewrites, Facebook at www.facebook.com/grahamewrites, our Facebook group Grahame Claire Reader Hangout at www.facebook.com/groups/GrahameClaire-ReaderHangout, Instagram @grahameclaire, or send us an email anytime at grahame@grahameclaire.com.

Follow us on BookBub at www.bookbub.com/authors/grahame-claire

Printed in Great Britain
by Amazon

24778939R00158